annie oakley's girl

rebecca brown

city lights
san francisco

Cover design by Rex Ray
Book design by Amy Scholder
Typography by Harvest Graphics

Library of Congress Cataloging-in-Publication Data

Brown, Rebecca, 1956-
    Annie Oakley's girl / by Rebecca Brown.
        p.   cm.
    ISBN 0-87286-279-9 : $9.95
    I. Title.
    PS3552.R6973A83   1993
    813'.54 — dc20   93-21777
                                                         CIP

City Lights Books are available to bookstores through our primary
distributor: Subterranean Company. P.O. Box 160, 265 S. 5th St.,
Monroe, OR 97456. 541-847-5274. Toll-free orders 800-274-7826.
FAX 541-847-6018. Our books are also available through library
jobbers and regional distributors. For personal orders and catalogs,
please write to City Lights Books, 261 Columbus Avenue,
San Francisco, CA 94133. Visit us at http://www.citylights.com

CITY LIGHTS BOOKS are edited by Lawrence Ferlinghetti and
Nancy J. Peters and published at the City Lights Bookstore,
261 Columbus Avenue, San Francisco, CA 94133.

ACKNOWLEDGMENTS

"Annie" was first published in *Mae West is Dead: Recent Lesbian and Gay Fiction*, Adam Mars-Jones, ed. (Faber and Faber, 1983). "Folie a Deux" was published in *The Jacaranda Review*, 1992. "A Good Man" was published in *Women on Women II*, Joan Nestle and Naomi Holoch, eds., (Dutton, 1993).

"The Joy of Marriage," "Love Poem," "The Death of Napoleon," and "Grief" were originally published in Britain in 1984. Copyright © Rebecca Brown.

"Grief" is for Megan Campbell.

Thanks to the MacDowell Colony for a residency in 1992 that gave me time and place to start the new book.

CONTENTS

ANNIE

Annie and I are the only women in the bar. She introduces me as her second cousin from Paris and says, "That's how come she cain't talk to y'all. Duddn't know a damn word o' English." This is her way of telling me to stay quiet so we can play one of our games. So I smile a lot and nod and laugh demurely when everyone else is laughing. I look at her with the look she's named my "sweetest lil' thang there ever wuz" face, which all the cowboys read as the ignorance of a foreigner, the innocence of a girl. Annie "translates" to me in the gibberish that passes for today's exotic language. They're always interested in my dress; do all the young girls in France (Tasmania, Russia, Italy, New

Jersey) dress like me? Annie will surprise me with something new, like, oh no, that I'm an exception where I come from too, a girl on the fringe, a slave princess, an exile, a Bohemian, a turkey herder. Or she'll just stick with the old standard, as she does today. "Yup. They're all jest lahk 'er, each 'n' ever' one."

Her clothes are wonderful. They're hanging in the wagon and it's evening. Annie's out fixing us stew and corn bread. I've just come back from bathing in the stream and, clean again, I drop my towel and squat down to straighten into even rows her pairs of boots and moccasins. I run my fingertips over the skins of lizard, snake, armadillo. I stand up and touch her clothes. I love the sturdy softness of the long-worn leather, the limp clean fur that gives to my touch, the heavy white muslin and thin white cottons. I love the thin dust-colored fringe across the back of her fancy jacket. I wrap the sleeves around me and bury my head inside where her shoulders fit. I close my eyes and breathe deep the smells of leather, of prairie, of western sky, of Annie.

Then her voice breaks in, "Come on now, honey, grub's up!" I slip into my jumpsuit and join her by the fire.

Our forks clink against the thin tin plates. The shape of the cups is clear and simple. Annie's stew is plain and coffee strong. She'd laugh if I tried to tell her about Hamburger Helper or Crazy Salt or beef-stew flavor packets. She'd be in stitches if I told her about Cremora, Coffee-mate, non-dairy coffee cream. When she asks me what I'm smiling about, I shake my head and tell her nothing. She wipes her mouth with her forearm and tells me stories about this place when no one had ever been here before. She's anxious that her elbow room is being invaded. She goes on and tells me about when the sky was bigger and the land stretched farther. Her voice is even and round and I vow to myself that I will never, *ever* breathe a word to her about Los Angeles. She spreads her arm beside her in a smooth arc as far as she can reach, to show me the horizon she remembers.

I wonder what she wonders when I go. I've explained to her as much as I can, or at least as much as I've told myself she can handle. I expect her to be puzzled, torn with curiosity, but she always seems completely satisfied. "Everybody's gotta saddle up and git sometimes," she comforts me. I tell myself that I should be the one to comfort her about the things in me that she can't know about. I remind her that there are places I go and things I do and people I am that she couldn't begin to understand. And sometimes, I must admit, I try to sound mysterious and tragic. But she looks at me clearly, waits for me to finish and tells me, "Well, a girl can only say what she can when she can, she jest gotta see about the rest."

I point out to her that the only things she knows about where I go and what I do when I get there are what I tell her. Then I ask her why she believes me. She looks hard at me, squints and wrinkles up her nose as if I were trying to talk to her seriously in gibberish. I try again, "Aren't you afraid one time I won't come back, that some day I will leave you?" Then she laughs her big laugh like it's a joke she's just understood. She winks and tells me, "Well, yew jest tell me whin, 'n' I won't look for y'."

My mother still has pictures of me in my cowgirl clothes. Every Christmas until I was eight or nine I got cowgirl clothes to replace the ones I'd outgrown. Skirts and vests and shirts and boots. Boots changed the fastest. I went through black pairs, brown pairs, beige pairs, even a pair of red ones. Somewhere early along the line I got a hat that was too big for me. The Christmas morning I ran down and found it, I put it on my head and it bumped into my glasses and nose. But I insisted on wearing it. I walked around that morning with my neck stretched and my head tilted back, looking down my nose and out at the world through the slit between my face and the dark line of my hat. It must have fallen off my head at least thirty times and stopped itself with the soft black and white string held together with the knot and wooden bead around my neck. Later that week my mother padded the inside of the hat to fit me. I wore it with the pride of a child who believes she has been mistaken for being older than she is.

Twice a year, in summer and right after Christmas, my family made the trip north to my grandparents' home in Oklahoma City. There were a couple of reasons why I didn't like the winter visit. First of all it meant I left almost all of my new toys and all of my friends and *their* new toys for a week in that most crucial and short-lived time when toys are still brand new. Plus I always considered the drive up a waste of precious time that could otherwise be spent in productive play. The "excitement of travel" and "gorgeous scenery," which my parents suggested I try to appreciate, were not my idea, as a preschool cowgirl, of a good time.

The summer visit, however, was an entirely different matter. I loved it: it was the high point of my year. And though I didn't know the word at the time, it was my pilgrimage. Because on one day of that summer week I was taken to "Westown" and on another to "The Cowboy Hall of Fame."

Westown, I now know, was an amusement park, a tacky little prefab money-maker. But I knew something different then; I knew it was a ghost town. But not quite even a ghost town, because somehow, by some miraculous dispensation, this town had stayed alive when all the rest had died. There were saloons with horses tied to posts in front, emporiums and general stores and every kind of Old West shop there could be. You could buy authentic frontier food, beef stew and corn bread, beans and white bread, molasses and grits, hamburgers and hot dogs. You drank sarsaparilla out of tin cups at the bar and your parents had coffee out of the same. Some people walked around looking like people anywhere, but some of them were dressed like true cowboys and cowgirls and Western gentlemen and ladies. I wore my cowgirl outfit and sometimes I'd pretend to get lost from my parents so I could walk around alone and pretend I lived there. I was sure some people thought I did live there because they'd always smile at me and say, "Well howdy, pardner." You could pay money and ride around a ring for ten minutes on Buffalo Bill's horse's grandson and get your picture taken. I did this every year. I remember vaguely wondering about this one year, when the horse was brown and I thought I remembered it being black, but my mother insisted that it was the same horse and I was just confused. Only last year did my mother show me the pictures of all the years together, and only then were my dark suspicions confirmed, when I saw myself on different sizes and shades of horses in the fuzzy black and white photos.

Each day ended with a trip to the Western Store when my father bought me one special thing, anything I wanted. All the stacks on the aisles were tall and I had to look up far. I was always scrupulous and careful. I weighed the pros and cons of everything I considered — a bronze belt buckle shaped like a bucking bronc, a holster or a pair of spurs, a hand-tooled leather belt that they could write my name on, a special red Westown bandanna, a cowboy tie, a band of feathers for my hat, a brand-new hat with red silk on the inside with the Westown logo written on it. The decision overwhelmed me. There was just too much to look at. It wasn't just the things you could buy — it was everything. There were pictures on the walls of famous cowboys and famous cowboys' horses. There were old rifles and samples of so many different kinds of barbed wire I couldn't count them. There were authentic horseshoes from famous cowboys' horses, Indian blankets, and headdresses. There were snakeskins hanging on parts of tree limbs and Wanted posters of famous outlaws under glass. There were wagon wheels and cattle brands and a life-sized wooden Indian.

There was old blue and silver Indian jewelry and beads and beaded moccasins. And after a whole day of Westown, this store and this decision were too much, like trying to decide between pecan and pumpkin and mincemeat pie or ice cream or sherbet or meringues for dessert, and all that *after* Thanksgiving dinner.

So I'd pick my choice, my heart trembling as I approached my father waiting at the counter, *Is this exactly what I want? Wouldn't the spurs be better?*, knowing that the decision was ultimate and irrevocable. When I finally handed my father whatever I'd decided on and he finally put it on the counter and then at last he finally paid the money, I was stricken first with regret — if I'd only waited one second longer maybe the strong, true, right revelation would have come and I would have *known* exactly and without a doubt what was the perfect thing to buy — then with relief, it was done, what I'd set out to do. I could check it off a list of things that I'd lived through.

I don't remember most of what I got, but I do remember a certain hat, though probably more because of what happened when I got it than for the hat itself. I left the store, heart pounding, palms sweating, as I held my father's hand. My hat felt sturdy and pretty on my head. My parents and I had just stepped off the wooden sidewalk in front of the store when — bang! — a shoot-out! Quick as a kid I spun down and took cover behind a sand-filled oil drum they'd converted into an ash can. I was proud of my cowgirl instincts and the skill I'd learned from sliding into home-plate at sandlot baseball games. The shooting continued for some minutes complete with loud-mouthed hollers and threats. "Yew cain't git me, yew yellow-bellied dog." "This town ain't big enuf fer th' two of us." I tried to stay completely still but I was worried about my parents. I looked around and couldn't see them. I squatted down farther in my hiding place and prayed to the little Lord Jesus that they'd escape all right. I also told him I was sorry for being proud about my cowgirl instincts.

When the fighting stopped and I heard the last body bite the dust, I stood up and saw three dead cowboys on the street. I looked frantically to find my mother and father. I saw a crowd of people standing in a loose semicircle on the street. I spotted my parents in the group just as they spotted me. My mother waved to me, then put her hand to her head. I put my hand to my head and realized my new hat had fallen off. I picked it up. It was dusty and I started to brush it off but then I didn't because I wanted to keep the dust to remember the shoot-out. I put my dusty cowgirl hat back on and started to run to my mother and father to see if they were OK, then I saw them start to clap. Everyone in the semicircle was clapping. I stopped to see why. They were all looking down the street so I did too. That's when I saw the three dead cowboys stand and smile and slap the dust from their chaps and hats and take their smart and often practiced bows.

Annie's silhouette against the evening sky: she's sitting on top of Cowgirl. She's wearing her fancy jacket and though it's still, the fringe on her sleeves, particularly near her elbows, stands out as if a breeze was blowing. Her two limp braids rest on her shoulders. She's facing the horizon, watching the sun sink in the west. Behind her the sky is brilliant orange and muted pink like an August peach. The land is flat except for a slight rise to her left. And just about the line where earth meets sky, a tiny star is twinkling. The sun rests, only a semicircle above the line, like the half coins in the March of Dimes display. Cowgirl's tail swishes and she raises her hoof then lowers it with a gentle soft "thoop." Dust kicks up around this foot, then settles light as the snow in a dollar-twenty snow scene in a bottle. I can just see the line that Annie's leg makes in her fancy skirt. Her holster rests against her thigh and I can see the curved line of her boot top and her naked calf below her skirt.

Saying these words is like speaking avocado, warm ripe juicy mango. "Appaloosa," "stirrup," "bay," "ride the open range." "Rope the herd," "meet at sundown," "Goodnight-Loving Trail." "Chaps" and "lassoes," "spurs" and "mares," "the coyote's cry at night." "Saddle up," "the lonesome trail," "the big wide open sky." "Rawhide leather," "Westward Ho!," "sleeping under stars." "Cattle rustler," "Remington," "six-shooter," "riding shotgun." "King Corral," "the fastest gun," "the sinking sun." "The West."

In my brother's eighth-grade shop class, he made me a leather holster. He cut the pieces by himself and shaped it to fit the new toy gun my father gave me on my birthday. My brother tooled my name on the holster and a picture of a cowgirl hat. I wore the holster to school, even without the gun. I fastened the belt around my skirt and carried my pencil bag where the gun would've fit. I was happy when I sat down and the holster hung down the side of my desk. I made a point of changing pencils every five minutes. I quick-drew my pencil bag and in a flash picked a new pencil to follow vocabulary dictation. After several pencil changes, my teacher told me I was making too much of a disturbance and would I be so good as to hang my holster in the cloakroom with the other children's things. So I went back and hung my holster with the lunch pails and sweaters and caps. I did it reluctantly, and made a point to "forget" and leave my pencil bag in the holster, so that when I "accidentally" broke the pencil I was using later that period, I had to go back to my holster and get another.

I wasn't allowed to wear it to school anymore after that, but every day when I got home, as soon as I changed into my play clothes, I put my holster on, complete with gun, and wore it very proudly.

Late that night, we ride into town and tie up Kid and Cowgirl by the Red-Eyed Jack Saloon. We walk in side by side, each of us pushing open one half of the swinging door. The whole saloon is quiet for some moments. Annie looks at me. I nod and she says, "Bring us a bottle of yer best whiskey, Jimbo. And set us up two shots." Jimbo looks at Annie, then looks at me, then back at her again. He hesitates. When he says to her, "Annie?" his voice is slow and tentative, like a kid unwrapping a present too good to be true and asking unbelievingly, "For me?" Annie grins and looks at him, then looks down the entire bar. Everything is silent and still except one cowboy who shifts uncomfortably in his seat. The sound of the creaking leather of his chaps startles him and he holds his breath. Annie scans the whole place, then looks at me and winks. She slips around on her barstool and faces the whole saloon. She spreads both her arms out wide, pauses, arms in the air, "Now is *this*," she slightly dips her arms, "what ya'll call a proper home-comin'?" Then the whole crowd bursts. Jimbo slaps his forehead, yells, "Shit fire damnation, Annie!" Cowboys whoop and jump from their chairs and run up to Annie and hug her. "Goddamn yew, Annie", "Sheeeee-ut, Annie's home!" Jimbo declares free drinks for all. Someone finds a harmonica and starts dancing. Cowboys toss their hats in the air and holler. Everyone slaps everyone on the back. When Annie introduces me they shake my hand and take off their hats and tell me, "Pleased t' meetcha," and later in the night they give me bear hugs. They give Annie capsule histories: Wally's with the railroads, Doc got married and Lou left town with some man from Chicago. Lucky ran to Mexico. Sally 'n' Jack got hitched up and took on Old Widow Whitley's place. And Jimmy's got his eye set on the Foster girl but his Momma 'n' Daddy don't know what they think of her. They ask her about Buffalo Bill and the travelling Wild West Show and she tells them everything.

Part of the floor gets cleared and all of us are dancing. The cowboys stamp their boots. Annie takes a turn with Jimbo, and I with some young hand just passing through.

Annie's skirt whirls around her and her braids fly. I watch her body spin through Jimbo's arms. The fringe strings on her jacket look alive and bright and I can pick out the sound of her boots clicking in the midst of all the rest. The night goes on forever. Cowboys collapse with happiness and booze. Little by little the cowboys leave, coming up to hug me and Annie again before they go saying, "Hon, we're so glad t' have y' back. How long y' stayin'?"

When the only ones left standing are Annie and me, we help Jimbo make the passed-out cowboys comfortable, remove their hats and cover them with blankets. When this is done Jimbo puts his arms around us, "Now y'all please stay as long as y' can. I had Jimmy take care o' Kid 'n' Cowgirl for y' 'n' Miz Burnley gotcha'll a room all ready." Then he looks at Annie and squeezes her. "I knew yew'd come back, Annie." The three of us step out on to the boardwalk and Jimbo offers to walk us over to Mrs. Burnley's Hotel, but Annie tells him we'll be just fine. When we walk out into the street alone, Annie takes her hat off and leans her head back to look up at the sky. I look at her face in the light of the moon then I look up at the giant sky. I hear her breathe in a big deep breath. Then I hear the sound of the stretch of her sleeve, the flap of the fringe on her jacket, and then a whoosh and she's flung her hat in the sky and I see her hat soar high. I see it climb, the brim all white with moon like a spine.

Every year there was one new statue. You saw the picture of it on the wall when you came in and I was always eager and excited to see it, and part of me wanted to run right to it and find it. I knew exactly where it would be, but part of me told myself to wait and save the best for last. I always wore a dress because it was inside. You went in and the air was cool and it felt very different from the hot heat of the blacktop of the parking lot. My grandmother came because she could, because it was cool and there were places to sit. I wore anklets and the last time I went I carried a little purse. It was a wooden box purse and it had two horses painted on it and they were running on the land.

You were quiet there and you walked slowly, reverently, you spent time poring over the index cards next to the exhibits behind the glass looking for words you knew. You tried to remember the names they read you or that you could read yourself: Cheyenne, Durango, Cimarron. There were maps and photos and scale models. There were simulated rooms that looked like schools and barber shops and stores. There were movies for free. In the new part there were black and white photo portraits of rodeo champs, and world record holders for bronco busting, cattle roping, bull riding. On both walls of a hallway there were pictures of Best All Around Cowboy for every year. There were big cards on the wall that told you history.

My grandmother read me the one about the pioneers. That always took her a long time because she told me about her father who was an Indian doctor. At home she showed me things the Indians gave him. She showed me a leather pouch, a blanket of wool, a pipe, a bag of charms, a round black pot, some arrowheads, a jar of painted sand, a necklace of colored beads.

The last thing in the Cowboy Hall of Fame was this year's statue. The last year I went there I got upset because this year's cowboy was just a cowboy singer and I wondered if he was really a true cowboy at all.

My first horse was a broom that I named Trigger. At first Trigger lived in the kitchen pantry where my mother kept her cleaning things, but then when Trigger became Trigger she moved into my bedroom. Sometimes my mother would borrow her, and when Trigger came back she'd have bits of cat hairs and tiny specks of wilted lettuce in her tail. So I'd brush her tail out and pat her neck. My brother attached long stringy reins to the metal hook that was Trigger's mouth. I rode Trigger all round the house. You could always hear me coming from my upstairs room because Trigger's tail always thumped the stairs on the way down. Sometimes I rode her so fast my hat would fall off and thank goodness it caught at the string around my neck. Whenever I needed to stop at the saloon for a snack I'd tie Trigger to the kitchen table. If no one was there I'd rustle up my own vittles, but if my mother was there she'd ask me, "What'll it be today, pardner, the usual?" and I'd say, "Yup," then she'd find me cookies or Twinkies or a piece of fruit. "How's Trigger today?" she'd ask, and I'd say, "Oh, just fine," and I'd tell her stories about the caves and plains and woods I'd ridden through that day, the Indians and outlaws I had met and saved her from or won over to our side.

The whole day's still. It's hot high noon; the sky's so blue it's white. But now I notice almost none of this. It's only in my memory that I will watch the sky get waved with heat, or see the fine dust film that mutes the color of the cacti, the curled-up snake that's sunning on the rock.

Because Annie and I are riding. We're tearing through the desert on an urgent, crucial errand. I don't know where we're going. We break the stillness. Somehow I feel that this is a violation. The hooves of both our horses pound. They run in rhythm, side by side. We travel in one huge cloud of dust. I can hear the gentle slap of our night packs on the horses' backs. I turn around from time to time to check my bundle's still intact, but Annie's tied it tightly. I grip one hand tight on the reins and clutch the saddle horn with the other. The reins relax in Annie's hands. She never kicks or slaps at Cowgirl. She can say most anything with a movement of her body or a click of her tongue; she moves forward, left or right, and Cowgirl knows. She grips her horse close with her thighs.

Beside me, Annie leans forward. Her braids stand out behind her. Her jacket billows up. "Annie!" I shout across to her, tightening my grip on the saddle horn, "Annie!" but she can't hear me above the pounding hooves. We move so fast the dry air hits me like a fan. Only it's hot, not cool. I think I'm beginning to feel burned from the sun. It's a healthy feeling, but I wonder if I've remembered to bring my sunglasses and Coppertone. The sun glints on her stirrup next to me and it flashes at me every time I look at her. I start coughing from the dust. I lift the loose bandanna around my neck and cover my mouth and nose to keep the dust out. The cloth smells dusty and I know that in just seconds I'll be uncomfortable from the moisture of my sweat and breath. I must hear something from her because when I turn she's already looking at me. She says something. I yell that I can't hear her then I point to my ear and shake my head, "no." I can see her laugh and nod. Then she points to her nose and chin, not covered by bandanna, then to me. Then she draws her pistol with a flick of her strong wrist. She stretches her arm into the sky and fires and fires again. She shakes her head with pleasure and points her face up to the sky and shouts a long "Hooooooo-eeeee!" of happiness. Her knees press Cowgirl and she races off ahead of me like I was standing still. She disappears in a cloud of dust. The only thing she leaves me with is the tail end of the whoop of joy behind her.

Annie tries to teach me how to cook above an open flame. She tries to teach me flapjacks, bacon, grits. The bottom half of everything burns and the top half is always raw. I burn my palm trying to grab the hot black handle and dump grease and batter into the fire. She tries to teach me to toast bread on a stick; the bread falls in the flames. I burn the coffee and scorch the beans. She doesn't even use tinfoil. I want to tell her about adjustable-flame gas burners, but I don't want to sound like I'm whining. She mixes things without a book. The only seasoning she'll use is salt. I think of woks and Cuisinarts and frozen vegetables. She brushes her teeth with baking soda. I sneak behind the wagon and press mint-flavored Crest on to my toothbrush. She's never tasted mint before. I don't want to confess.

I'm thrilled. We're in a stagecoach. I'm wearing gloves and button boots and a long-sleeved dress with lace around the sleeves and high neck collar. I have a hat and veil on. "Now jest who you tryin' t' keep outta there anyhow, honey?" she asks and laughs out loud, then slaps her ungloved hands against her knees. "Jeee-umpin' Jehosefat!" she nearly shouts and looks out the window beside her. "Looks all little bitty when y' got a window 'round it." She leans out the window and shouts at the scout who rides his horse beside us. "How's thangs out there, Willy?"

"Jest fine, Annie."

"Well, I tell yew," she hollers back, "it shore looks dif'ernt from in here, Willy-boy!"

"Now doncha fret there, Annie, ain't nobody gonna pull nothin' over on y'!"

She smiles back and keeps staring out the window until gradually her lips are straight. She leans her elbow out the window ledge and puts her chin in her hand. I watch her quiet profile against the landscape moving fast and flat behind her. She's always ridden on horseback outside the coach before. The brim of her hat casts a shadow down most of her face. She's wearing her fancy skirt and fancy jacket and a bright pink shirt I bought for her when I bought my dress and boots. On the shelf above her, our two suitcases; her beat-up leather bag with the rounded, well-scratched metal corners, and my ladies' light, sky-blue

American Tourister.

I find a lacy handkerchief in the beaded bag beside me and gently dab at my neck and upper lip and forehead.

Then I pull out my embroidery and try to teach her how to stitch.

Tonight I undo Annie's braids. She sits facing the boudoir mirror in our hotel room, in what is now a ghost town in Nevada. I sit behind her working on her hair. She's tied the bottom of the braids with leather. The braids are tight and smooth and gold with sun. I undo one and then the other, untying them at the bottom and separating the three even groups of hair in each. Then I shake them evenly and brush her hair out straight and all together. Her hair is wavy from the constant braids but I can tell it's naturally straight. I brush firmly, starting at the very top of her part and continuing down in strong hard strokes the whole length of her hair. I brush the sides above her temples and underneath the back of her head. Her hair parts naturally in the middle and back. I expect it to be coarse, but it feels like a baby's.

I brush and brush until her hair is smooth and soft as silk, and shiny. It looks like still gold water. Then I look up at the mirror to catch her eye and ask her what she thinks. But her eyes are closed. She's sitting up straight, asleep. I study her face and notice something missing that I'd come to believe was always there. It's something she can't tell me.

But Annie prefers the open range to hotel life. She likes to sleep in whistling distance of Cowgirl. "Thangs weren't always lahk this now," she tells me. It's hard for her to break the habits that she made when things weren't tame.

I've stopped telling her to relax, to let other people care for Cowgirl, to cook her meals, and wash her things behind her. I think perhaps her work *is* her true pleasure.

I started riding lessons when I was five. In the family album there's a picture of me, tiny and blonde, my light blue glasses with the pointy frames slipped down to the end of my nose. I'm sitting on a huge brown horse. My feet reach way above the middle of the horse's back. My head doesn't reach as tall as the horse's. I remember my seriousness in posing for this photo. I refused to wave or smile because I didn't want it to look like a game. I wanted it to look like this was something I did every day, quiet and serious.

The horses I rode had these names: Penny, Marshal, Slim, and Little Bit. Blackie, Kit, Friskie, Nick. Old Tom, Old Paint, Old Gray, Brandy. Roger, Ho-boy, Loosa, Beaut. Carson, Big Boy, May.

I'm given priority seating at the Wild West Show. I sit between a railroad tycoon and a meat packer from Chicago. The only other women there are wives or gentlemen's companions. I'm wearing a plastic photo ID on my blouse. I assume that this allows me access, along with the other VIPs and invited guests, to the private quarters and refreshment rooms. But oddly enough, I'm the only one with a tag. And even more oddly, no one seems to notice that I've got one. I watch for Annie through a pair of opera glasses. Of course, she is the star. She introduces all the acts and takes care of people before they hit the ring. And I know, though we don't see this, that she also acts as everybody's friend, encouraging, counseling, helping out. The people around me in the box discuss the show with terms like "quaint" and "rugged." I hear myself tittering with them at their urban jokes and holding my teacup with my little finger extended. When Annie races out of the waiting stall and charges into the ring, six-gun firing, I hear the whole crowd gasp then cheer. The people in the booth I'm in clap evenly and nod to one another and say, "charming," "lovely," "marvelous." After the show, when the others in the box tell me of their oil deals in Texas, their railroads in Ohio and their newest warehouse in the city, they ask me, roundaboutly, how I'm with them in the box. I nod and tell them, "I am an acquaintance of Miss Oakley."

This time when I come back, I bring her a present. Annie unwraps the boxes and laughs at the paper with the flapper-girl designs. When she first pulls out her newly laundered fancy skirt and jacket, she doesn't recognize them, then she does. "Well, land o' goshen, honey, what'd y' do t' these thangs?"

"I had them dry-cleaned, Annie."

She looks at me and nods with that tentative nod you give when you feel like you should say, "yes," but you don't really know quite why.

"And weather-proofed," I add proudly.

She looks at me and squints.

"Feel that?" I take her hand and rub it over the newly treated leather. "That'll protect it from the rain and keep it stronger."

"Uh-huh," she says, her face still puzzled. She brings the jacket to her face, looks at it closely, sniffs it.

"Never needed it before," she says.

I nod, "I know, but this is better."

Annie takes the skirt and jacket and the three special blouses from the box. She gingerly places them out flat on the table and looks them over again. "Hmmm-mm," she mutters.

The ladies at the dry-cleaner had been impressed. They'd ooh-ed and aah-ed at the leather and fine handwork. I'd told them they'd been in the family for many years and asked them to be extra careful. I'd hoped Annie would be pleased they looked like new. I was.

This night when I wake up it's not a nightmare; it's a storm. When my eyes spring open I see Annie sitting by the bed, polishing her boots in the dim light of the oil lamp. When I sit up, she looks at me and I ask, "What are you doing? Why are you awake?" The canvas cover of the wagon heaves with blowing air. Lightning cracks and thunder interrupts her voice.

"I thought y' might wake up and git afeared, so I thought I'd be here in case y' did."

I look at her and I don't know what to say.

She looks away from me then tries to sound buoyant and matter-of-fact, "Besides, I hadda polish these dang thangs."

I pretend that I accept all this for what it is and think nothing more. I close rny eyes as if I were asleep and listen to her breathe, and the swish and buff of her hands at work beneath the sound of rain.

We're out in the open and it's almost fall. I try to read in the changing light of the open fire. The only sounds are the crack of flame and the soft wet sound of Kid and Cowgirl chewing, then the sound of Annie's boots walking back from checking on the horses. Her boots scrape across the rough dry ground.

"Nice night," I say as she returns to the fire and stretches her hands to the warmth.

She nods and looks into the flame, but I don't think she's looking at anything.

"How's Kid and Cowgirl?"

"Oh, fine . . ." She nods. Her voice is tired. I watch her as she sits down by the light. She stoops, puts her hands on her thighs, then on the ground beside her. She exhales as she finally sits then breathes in loud. She brushes back the hair that's fallen in her face then rubs her eyes. She pulls her hand down over her whole face, stretching her cheeks, then she rubs the back of her neck and twists her head. Her eyes are closed and I can't tell if it's the shadow of flame or if it really is bags under her eyes, and wrinkles at the outer edges. And I tell myself that now I will tell her. I say very softly, "Annie?" But Annie doesn't hear me.

There's a feeling you get when you're away and you think, "If only I was there . . . if only I was with . . ." and you look forward to it and you save up things for when you are. You think, "If I was there, if I was with . . . then I'd say this and this . . ." But then you are there, truly and at last, and you think, "This is what I wanted. This is when I can say those things . . ." but something happens and you can't or don't say them. Then you tell yourself that things aren't what you hoped they would be. You still can't speak and now you wonder if you'd have been better off never to have learned this other meaning of "alone." If it would have been better always to have been able to look forward, or back, and think, "If only . . . when . . ."

But I don't not miss her when I go: I do.

The next time I come back I tell her, "Annie, I want you to come with me. This time. When I go away."

Annie looks straight at me, smiles, tells me, "OK, pardner."

My favorite show was "Have Gun Will Travel." The second was "Gunsmoke," then "Bonanza," and "Batt Masterson." Next, "The Rifleman." You knew what day of the week it was by who you'd get to watch. And the next day the playground buzzed with recaps. We talked about everything, debated points of character, how things could have turned out, "if only . . ." We tried to top each other by saying how early on we knew just who'd done it and how it was going to end. We guessed about the fate of future episodes. We screened our own scenarios and we fantasized a meeting of all the greats together — all of them

— Batt Masterson, Matt Dillon, Palladin, the entire Cart-wright family. I wanted to be there. I started all these talks.

"Tarnation, honey, I never saw a damn thang like it." Annie's standing on the balcony of my thirty-second floor apartment suite in Manhattan. She's looking out at the city. I push aside clothes in my closet to make room for her things.

Annie and I walk the city for weeks. Some parts of it she'll recognize, or tell me what used to be at this address. She reminisces about performing in the Wild West Show with Buffalo Bill at Madison Square Garden. She can't believe how the city's grown, how many cars and lights, the height of buildings, noise and speed of everything. She loves the accents that she hears in delis, clothes stores, on street corners. But her favorite things are movies.

The first Western I take her to see is *High Noon*. We have a great time and start haunting old movie houses and taking in all the Westerns. Pretty soon, that's all we do. We see *Shane, The Great Train Robbery, The Gunfighter, Gunfight at the OK Corral, The Covered Wagon, Man With a Gun*. At first she laughs at them, she can't believe we take them seri-ously. But after a while she's fascinated. We have to see one every night. Every night when we hit a theater, Annie dresses in her cowgirl best and I in something chic and new. And though sometimes we get glances, this is the city and people don't look twice.

After a while she gets restless during the day. The city is too crowded and fast and loud for her. We buy a video cassette machine so she can always have a Western on hand.

I start to get concerned. Is she unhappy? I throw a huge party and invite all the most interesting people I know. This is the first night we don't go see a Western. I hope that she'll be happy. The night goes beautifully. My friends all think she's great and we have fun. Annie tells stories of her growing up, her early career, the nation's adolescence. Everyone's entertained. "Oh, Annie," they say, "you should write a book." Everyone thinks her clothes are just right and ask her where she found them.

Late that night we start a hand of cards. I urge Annie to challenge everyone to poker and she does. While I refill my guests' daiquiris, Bloody Marys and Perrier-and-limes, Annie measures out her own shots of whiskey. They all lose to her and love it. At the end of the night they owe her millions, but Annie says, "Y'all have already paid me more 'n enuf in kindness."

Early that morning when the last guest is gone, and Annie and I are emptying ashtrays and wiping up spilled booze and dip, I thank her and tell her that this is the best party I've ever given. I say, "I haven't had this much fun since I was a kid." I tell her and she smiles. "They loved you, Annie," I nearly shout.

"Well, yer friends are most obligin'."

"Come on, Annie," I insist, "it's *you*. You're the greatest. There's something about you. It's . . . everybody loves it . . ."

"Yer very, very kind."

Annie kneels over a spot in the carpet trying to pick out

bits of crushed-up macadamia nut. I look at the bottoms of her boots then up at her cowgirl hat. I step over to her, take the hat off her head and put it on mine as I flop down on the couch beside her.

"Hey, Annie, do you like it here?"

She continues what she's doing. "Yup. Enuf — "

"Come on, Annie, what do you really think of this — well, all of this — ?" I sweep my arms out wide though she's not watching me.

When she answers me she's still looking at the floor. "Well, I think . . ." she hesitates, "yer here . . ." she hesitates even longer, "so I like it."

I'm so busy with my train of thought I almost miss her meaning. In fact, part of me tries to miss her meaning, but the part that doesn't imagines itself kneeling down with her and touching her, holding her in its arms. But the other part hastens away from that, pretends that things never mean anything more than they seem to. And this part stays frozen, seated, nervously pats Annie's hat down tighter on my head and tells her:

"Annie, ol' girl, I think you're gonna be a hit."

When Annie looks up at me from her chore, I put my index finger to my lips, look out the window at the city getting pink with light, and say, before the one part of me tells the other part to change its mind, "Yeah, I think you could be *very, very* big."

I try to explain the finer points to her. But she's never even heard of most of these things. "A self-fulfilling prophecy is when you say something and just the act of saying it is magic; it makes it happen. Foreshadowing and symbols are names you give to things in art, but they happen in life as well. Are you listening, Annie? Sometimes I look at you when we're happiest and that's when they come on me and I wish we weren't happy. Because once you have something, you want it. And you still keep wanting it when you can't have it." Her face is curious and calm and puzzled. She genuinely doesn't hear me.

I tell her, "Dear Annie, one day we'll wish none of this had happened. There's a price you pay for having what you want. You pay with the wanting that stays on after you stop having. You can want everything, but you can't *have* everything."

I explain these things to her when she's asleep. I tell myself I'm practicing and when I finally get it right, I'll tell her straight, out loud.

Your first lessons you have to ride around a ring. They teach you how to walk and trot and canter. You have to do everything with everyone and that is no adventure. I always wanted to be let out on my own and ride free through the woods that started just fifty yards or so from the lesson corral. I'd never been in there but I saw where the trail went in and you couldn't see any more. I saw people ride in there sometimes. Older people, people that worked there who always wore boots and hats. I wanted to go into those woods by myself and ride and ride and ride. One lesson I brought a canteen and a sandwich in my brother's Boy

Scout bag and wore them on my belt because that day, I swore to myself, when the teacher wasn't looking, I would go. I'd gallop to the woods and follow that path as far as it went and then go farther. I'd ride and ride and ride. I'd spend the night in the woods and live off nuts and berries. I'd drink water from streams and tie my horse to a tree and sleep by a dying fire. I'd meet up with some cowboys and they'd show me how to get to the open plains and I'd go and find a cowtown and I would visit there, and go from cowtown to cowtown, meeting people and living like a cowgirl.

Annie's signing autographs at Saks. We've timed it so the release of her authorized biography coincides with the arrival of the special line of new fall fashions — Annie Oakley Western Wear. Annie sits on the ladies' sidesaddle which they've rigged up on a chair and chats with customers and buyers. Saks fashion models dressed in cowgirl Western wear scurry in the crowd around her. They smile a lot and offer free champagne and hors d'oeuvres, and turn to show the catchy lines their outfits cut. They all wear hats and underneath their hats their hair is permed or streaked or blow-dried. They make sure each buyer gets the right amount of time to say hello to Annie, joke with her, buy her book. Then they subtly, persuasively, draw people away to buy some Western clothes. Annie laughs and sometimes she does a quick-draw show or spins a tight, fast lasso. The whole crowd loves her, listens rapt to her stories about the range, six-shooters, the setting sun. Clearly she is a hit.

They laugh at every joke she tells and sigh at every story. When they say things to her they sound sincere and grateful and loving. She is their heroine. They're all in love with her.

I stand apart, sipping my champagne by the escalator. I keep one eye on everything around her while I pretend to enjoy the chit-chat with the customers. When it gets near time to close the crowd thins out, the "cowgirls" begin to go back to their rooms and change. Annie's pretty much left alone. I duck into the ladies' room and when I return I see her talking to one of the workers undoing the display. They're laughing with each other and Annie's face is live with animation. I watch her tell her story for some minutes, then when the story gets too long I walk over and tell her briskly, "You don't have to do this anymore. You've put in your time."

Annie's face falls. The worker snaps back to the job.

That evening in our hotel suite after our bags are packed for our night flight to L.A. we start to dress for dinner. *High Noon* plays on the VCR. We aren't watching it but we don't dare turn it off and listen to the silence. Annie's pulling on her boot and I'm holding her pair of spurs when I say, "All right, Oakley, spill it."

She stops, her leg outstretched, the boot poised at an angle in the air. She looks at me and doesn't say anything. I step over to the tube and turn the volume all the way down.

"Go on," I start into her, "tell me how much you love having all those good clean folks ooh-ing and aah-ing over you. Tell me about that precious little janitor sighing up at you. Christ."

Then I clasp my free hand over my heart and say in my best fake sweet starstruck voice, "She's even more wonderful than I imagined. Oh gosh, oh gee. She's so — so — good." I stare up toward the ceiling mocking the romanticism of the people I'd seen that day. I stand still a second then fling my hands out like I'm trying to strike at something. "Jesus Christ, you made me sick today. I mean it. You're something else. You really are something goddamn else." I pause. "But hell, what am I being upset about?" I shrug my shoulders and smile my sweetest smile. "You're only giving them what they want." I raise my voice in imitation again. "Gosh, were things really like that? Gee, Annie, you're a dream come true. Boy, Annie. I feel like I can really talk to you." I catch my breath and clench my free hand into a fist. I walk to one end of the room then back, tossing the spurs back and forth from one hand to the other. I turn and face her directly. I look at her a second, and try to make my voice sound calm and matter-of-fact but I can't. I say with all the spite I can, "You fucking whore."

Annie's eyes widen and her mouth opens slightly with sadness and surprise. She looks like she's about to cry. I feel horrible. I know I'm wrong. I want to take back everything but I'm too afraid and proud to change my mind so I raise my voice and spit out at her, "But what did I expect? You're Annie Fucking Oakley. Annie Fucking Jesus Oakley. You only give them what they want — "

Then Annie interrupts me. It's the only time she ever interrupts me in her life. She says, "Yew said yew wanted them to like me. Yew said I should be like that. Yew said that's why *yew* liked me."

Then she's quiet. Then she says, "I only did this fer yew."

I don't know what to say to her. I look back at the movie and watch Gary Cooper mime a passionate appeal to my patriotism. I walk over to the set and turn the volume up full blast and look at Annie, knowing we won't shout above the movie.

On my way out the door I remember the spurs and spin round and hurl them at the set. I slam the door and hurry away before I can hear anything else.

I leave a message at the desk for them to call for Annie when the limo arrives and to tell her that I'll meet her at the airport.

I walk uptown. I don't go in any bars, but do pass one I glance at. The name of it's "The Dude Ranch." Three blocks farther on I see "The Bucking Bronc," but I try to walk past without giving it a second look. I see a couple in cowboy hats and try to see if they're really from out West or just New Yorkers trying to be chic.

I try to remember how long those bars have been here.

Annie's drinking a strawberry daiquiri in the airport bar when I find her. Just as I walk up to her I hear our flight announced. We're going to Los Angeles. I throw a twenty on the table and help her stand. I see she's crying. "There,

there," I say as I help her up, pretending it's just the departure that's made her cry.

In the first class compartment Annie orders daiquiri after daiquiri. She experiments with different flavors — banana, peach, lime. I don't know whether to pray that they do show a Western, or to pray that they don't. We're on our way to Hollywood to negotiate the rights to her biography. She's never been drunk before.

"I'z afraid yew wudn't be comin' back." It's the first word she's said to me since I found her in the bar.

"I told the clerk I'd meet you at the airport."

"But I didn't know if yew meant it. All the stuff y' always used t' tell me 'bout leavin'. I was just tryin' t' figure it out."

I close my eyes and remember, with shame, things I'd tried to tell her, but I can't remember anything clearly, just vague words and unconnected thoughts — something about self-fulfilling prophecy, trying to sound mysterious and tragic, foreshadowing, the seed of doubt. I flinch when I think of what I've cooked up and fed to her.

Her eyes are closed beneath her hat which tips awkwardly over her face. I take her hat off and put it in the cabinet above us. Then I smooth her hair down. I hold her hands and look at them. I wipe her face and hold the tissue as she blows her nose. I feed her her lime daiquiri.

"Annie?" I whisper, "Annie? Annie?" I don't know what else to say.

She's mumbling things I can barely make out. I wave away the stewardess who offers us the movie earphones. Then I think I hear Annie say, "I don't belong . . . I miss the gang . . . cain't we go back? . . . please, cain't we go back? . . ." I wipe the moisture off her face then hold both her hands in mine. Annie sleeps. I don't think of anything. The lights go dim and the cabin screen gets light and I see the camera pan across the great vast open plains, a classic Western sunset. Just as the cowboys start across the screen, I close my eyes and thank God I can't hear the sound track. The cabin air feels cold and dry. I hear the chilled air coming in. Then I know that I will send her back. And I'll awake alone in California.

But I don't know when in the night she'll go. So I don't know if this is a dream I have or something I see that happens when she goes back:

Annie's riding Cowgirl. They're tearing through the desert with a leather pouch for the Pony Express. Her just-cleaned jacket gets blown with dust. Annie's getting winded. The sun is hurting her eyes. Her hand that grips the saddle horn lets up and she pats all her pockets, searching for what I can only guess must be her sunglasses. Her body jerks up and down on Cowgirl. There's nothing smooth or graceful between them.

And though I know she can't remember me, I wonder if she does because the look on her face is a mixture that's strange — a thing poised taut between a type of fear, and boredom, and something not at all unlike nostalgia.

THE JOY OF MARRIAGE

We go to the country for our honeymoon. I've chosen a small isolated cottage far from everything because I want us to be alone at last after our huge wedding and reception.

We unpack in the tiny room, and as I lift our empty clothes from our suitcases I'm suddenly overcome with desire for you. I try my hardest to be patient and then, when the suitcases are empty, you let me kiss you. I rush to unbutton my blouse and drop my slacks and give myself to you when I hear a car pull up outside and you say, "Don and Martha," as I'm pulling your hand over my bare breast, "It must be Don and Martha." You pull yourself away from me and dash for the window. I follow you and see outside a large black Rolls Royce. The chauffeur has just opened the car door and a woman's beautiful leg is starting out of the car. She and a man get out of the car and wave to us. "It *is* Don and Martha," you say eagerly, waving back to them. Reluctantly I wave too, careful to hide my naked breasts with my free hand.

I lag behind you, pulling up my slacks as you usher Don and Martha inside. They address me by name and hug me. Martha helps me zip my fly. "You remember Don and Martha, don't you, dear?" "Of course, of course," I say, fumbling with the button at my waist. And, though they remind me of lots of your friends, I can swear I've never met either of them before. Martha squeezes my hand and whispers to me, "I'm so happy for you." You and Don tell the chauffeur to pull the car around to the back.

As I'm slipping my hands into my sleeves, wondering how we're ever going to feed the four of us, the doorbell chimes. I'm startled to hear such a majestic signal, especially in a little one-room cottage like this. I'm wondering what to make of this when a butler answers the door and in rush two men in tuxedos. "Bill! John!" you cry with joy. You give them handshakes and hugs. "Hey there, you old son of a gun," John says as he slaps you on the back. Bill and John step toward me, each pecking me on the cheek with a kiss. John winks at me as I'm fumbling with my blouse, and whispers, "Looks like we've caught you at an awkward time."

A servant carries in four matching pieces of leather luggage. I turn around to see if there's any way we can fit it all under the bed, but, when I turn, I don't see the small bedroom you and I had unpacked in, but a grand staircase straight out of a thirties musical. My fingers go numb with shock as I'm buttoning my blouse.

The butler starts carrying Don and Martha's suitcases upstairs and behind me I feel a maid slipping me into a housecoat. She guides me up to a bedroom on the second floor where evening clothes for me are laid out on the bed. She leaves me alone to dress, and after she closes the door behind her, I hear the doorbell downstairs ringing and ringing.

I don't know how much time has passed, but when I go downstairs, it's lively with noise. A doorman ushers me into the dining room and before me stretches a table so long I can't see the end of it. I stand at the door and peer over the half-filled plates and half-empty bottles, cloth-covered bread rolls, and silver-covered dishes. The brilliance of all the silver glitters at me. The tablecloth is long and white. The people alternate between fine black suits and pastel dresses. I don't see anyone I know. You sit at the end of the table close to me, and just above the edge of the chair I can see the back of your head.

Then I'm sitting next to you and I realize I've just missed dinner. My stomach growls as the servants clear the plates. I hold your hand under the table. Just as I'm starting to caress your palm, you stand up to deliver a toast. The toast you deliver is for me, for our happiness in marriage. Everyone stands and toasts me. They clink their glasses and smile at one another and tip their glasses back. I search the empty place-setting in front of me for a glass, but there's not a drink in sight. Right then a corps of cooks wheels out a tremendous cake with our names, yours and mine, written on it. You sit down and I think how long it will take to serve everyone from this huge cake. Under the table, I slide my hand up your thigh, slowly, as tantalizingly as I can, and just when I feel you want me, and I'm about to touch you, you stand up to propose another toast. Embarrassed, I stare into the empty place setting in front of me and try not to listen as you talk about the joy of marriage. I hope the guests supply their own reasons why I'm blushing.

After dinner, some of the guests drift into the billiards room and smoke cigars, and some of them drift into the parlor and fan themselves and eat after-dinner mints. Others dance in a tremendous ballroom where a small orchestra plays waltzes. I wander from room to room, lost, looking for you. When I open the door to the study, the lights are out and someone says "Sshhh" and hastily closes the door behind me. It smells like smoke and whiskey and sweat. On a screen in the back of the room, a movie is flickering. It's a sex movie and I'm embarrassed to see it. I turn to leave but someone's crowded in behind me and when I look for the door I can't see it. I turn back to the screen and, in horror, I realize that I recognize one of the figures in the movie: it's you. Then I recognize the other one: it's me. I'm about to shout a protest or lunge for the light switch and put a stop to this when I hear your voice and you're saying, "Here comes the best part," in the same tone as if you were describing "Old Faithful" from a Yellowstone National Park vacation home-movie. Then, you slow the camera down and I hear your voice soothingly narrating our love-making with move-by-move coverage. I watch and listen, rapt, as you describe us. Then, when I feel the movie is about to near its end, I close my eyes and put my hands over my ears in shame.

The next thing I know, all the lights are on and everyone is clapping. The smoke is heavy in the room and I hear folding metal chairs scrape against the floor as people stand up to leave. Men roll their sleeves back down and slip back into their jackets. The few women who are there dab their necks and foreheads with handkerchiefs. I try to leave quietly, but someone catches me, shakes both my hands and says, "You were marvellous, just really marvellous." A young woman with tears on her cheeks comes up to me, stares deeply into my eyes, hugs me close, whispers, "Beautiful, beautiful, beautiful." A middle-aged man with a five o'clock shadow grabs my hand and murmurs "All I can say is thank you. You have no idea how much this has meant to me." Then he shakes his head as if he can't find any words.

When I look over at you, you're smiling broadly, shaking hands with someone. Then you lean over the projector and patiently show him how it works.

Our honeymoon house is full of people and they just

keep staying on and on and on.

In the evenings women wear satin and chiffon and men wear dark tuxedos. In the afternoons everyone wears tennis clothes and everyone looks sleek and tanned and has beautiful muscle tone. Some people play tennis and some people play polo in the field that's materialized on the east lawn, or go yachting in the lake that appeared here mysteriously. Some people just play cards and sit on the veranda drinking cool, iced drinks.

I wander from game to game, looking for you. Everyone always tells me I've only missed you by an instant.

Soon I take to walking around with my clothes only half-buttoned, half-zipped, because I'm so eager to be with you when I find you, and you're so hard to find and you move so fast that I want to be sure that, when I do find you, I won't have to spend time unbuttoning and unzipping. Eventually, I take to walking around completely naked.

Every night after dinner there is dancing and drinking and cigar smoking and the movie. Every night it's the same film which you call *The Joy of Marriage*. The first part of the film is of our wedding and reception. This part shows the countless happy party-goers you invited to "share in the joy of the day of our communion," as you put it then. I guess that the popularity of this part of the film is due to the fact that some members of the audience had been our wedding and reception guests and enjoy seeing themselves on film. We had packed out the cathedral, and then we'd packed out half the Fairmont. You and I had had an understanding about the social necessity of doing all this partying:

we reasoned it wouldn't be too much because we'd follow it with our secluded honeymoon. One scene in this part shows a shot of the bridesmaids standing right outside the cathedral door. I'm the diminutive figure in white, and though the print is perfectly clear, it's hard to tell exactly who the dark squatting figure that catches the brilliant blue garter I throw is. Oddly enough, you too are in this sequence, crouching in front of us, then squatting and clicking the same still camera you're carrying as you scurry about for the best angle. I don't know who got this footage. But in the last few frames before the scene change, you throw your arm around me and point me to the camera, press your cheek to mine and smile broadly. You wave to the movie camera with your free arm, which holds your still camera. Then the movie camera zooms in to our two faces. This shot fades into the second part of the film, the part that gives the film its title, *The Joy of Marriage*; our two bodies familiar and comfortable and kind with each other.

Gradually, word gets around, and the movie becomes so popular that it draws the crowds from the other evening activities. Gradually, too, the whole crowd increases and we have to move the film-showing into the theater that's appeared in the basement.

All the people who see the film come up to me and tell me how sweet I am in it. They also tell me they've never seen a pair like us and tell me we remind them of Valentino and what's-her-name, Bogart and what's-her-name, Gable and what's-her-name. I think they mean me to take these things as compliments.

Eventually, everyone is in the theater from morning to night and you run the film continuously. You run the film for weeks, months. Sometimes I try to make my way over to you and talk to you, but, with all the expansion, you've had a projection booth built and you're sealed inside. Once I get close enough to tap on the glass, but either you can't see me in the dark or you just choose not to respond to me.

After a while, you sense some restlessness on the part of the audience because, arty, strange, and beautiful as the film is, even the most interested audience tires of infinite reruns. So you decide to do a retrospective show and run all the films you've ever made that led up to this film.

This night you show films of you and all of your ex-lovers. You preface the progam with an introductory statement, the theme of which is an homage to me, a grand testament to our love. Your tone is that of an evangelical sinner saved by grace, and your showing of these films is your confession. There are countless films, and we watch them for hours and hours and hours, starting with your first lover when you were fifteen. The print is Technicolor and everything looks fake. Then you show a succession of lovers before me, black and white, color, a couple of slide shows, a multimedia presentation. Then you end with the three other lovers you had during our engagement. These last three films are very painful to me. Then these three are followed by footage of you speaking into the camera, confessing the error of your ways and sharing with your audience how much you've learned, especially about faith and patience, through me. You look so innocent and sincere, and this makes me realize that this is one of the reasons I love you. The soft lighting behind you makes you look like a novitiate. I hear several soft sighs in the audience.

But much as I am drawn into these films, I keep glancing back up at the projection booth to see if I can see more than the orange nub of your cigarette burning above the machines.

After the confession footage, you again show *The Joy of Marriage.* The applause following this is deafening. Clearly, everyone is moved by the honesty with which you present your difficult struggle. People admire you and identify with you. I think I could even say they love you. Yes, they do, they idolize you.

After this showing several people come up and draw me aside by my naked arm and tell me first how moved they were by the presentation. How proud I must be to know you, to be part of you, they say. They ask me to tell them what you're "really like," no really, what you're *really* like. Their eyes are greedy and full of desire. Naked as I am, I find myself sweaty and hot and shaky, not the way I used to feel when I used to rip my clothes off in desire for you during our engagement, but in a different way. People offer me money to tell them about you and I tell them I can't. They sigh and say how good and noble it is of you to tell me to keep our special, private selves to us alone. They tell me I'm sweet for not selling out and telling the delicious secrets of our honeymoon.

And this is our honeymoon, isn't it? A bit extended, sure;

a few more honeymooners, sure, but it is, as I tell myself repeatedly, *our honeymoon.*

During the day sometimes I leave the showings and walk around and try to imagine the place before it grew, before the theater, when I still felt like wearing clothes. When I walk into a room now, I feel invisible or, rather, I feel fully clothed; that is, no one comments on my exposed flesh, though I feel heat and chill and the brush of others' bodies against my body more.

And at night when I go back to our room alone, as I have done since the first day we arrived here, I dream of a small cottage in the country, a honeymoon cottage. And I dream of you, despite the fact that I've forgotten what you look like in 3-D, the flesh.

Sometimes I even prowl around the house and grounds to see if I can find you. Because, though everyone else thinks you are with me, I know that that's a lie. I wander through the gardens where the cool night air tingles on my skin. I wander through the rooms and even through the theater.

You must take a break some time. And this is when I hope to catch you some time, alone, off guard, without your loving audience, without the perfect face you are on film.

FOLIE A DEUX

In the interest of security, we agreed to put out your eyes and burn out the insides of my ears.

This made sure we were always together. Each of us had something the other didn't have, something the other needed, and each of us knew exactly what the other needed and how to take care of the other. I read the newspaper to you and the *New Yorker* and your mail and the lyric sheets to our new albums. I held your hand everywhere we walked. I told you when you had on stripes and paisley. You wrote me notes about things on the radio. You described cadences of the new records we bought and tapped out their melodies on my thighs when you were sitting next to me.

You wrote me notes about all the things I couldn't know about anymore. You took care of my phone calls.

I learned to read your lips perfectly and worked on my "strong silent type" image that could excuse me from taking part in conversation much. You got very good at sensing physical presences and only bumped into things infrequently. You got new glass eyes and tinted glasses. You cultivated an "imaginative genius" image that acted as your cover for your staring into space and missing out on physical details. You held my arm casually and easily so it looked like we were just young lovers, comfortable and excited and eager to be with each other constantly. We figured out Morse code between us. I read the book aloud to you; you tapped it out to me. What others would think was a nervous habit or a desire for physical contact was really the secret and necessary and only form of communication common to both of us.

We took things slowly and carefully. We stayed home alone together for a long time until we thought we were normal enough to get by outside and normal enough so no one could tell. We didn't want anyone to know; it was our secret.

You had told your public you were going to lock yourself up with your new work for a while. The day of your return concert was the first day we had left the house. We went to the Center to practice. I told the stagehands they must keep the piano and bench exactly where they were: "Not a fraction of an inch off," I said. "Acoustics," you said. They obliged. It was the first time we'd spoken with or seen anyone who'd known us before. We were each a little scared, but we pulled it off just fine.

We asked them to leave (you needed to be alone with the instrument), and they left. Then you practiced. You practiced getting from me, behind the curtain, to the piano. We walked through it together, first you holding my arm, then without my arm, me walking beside you, then by yourself. After several times you could do it perfectly. You didn't touch the keys.

That night I was with you until right before you went on. I let you go, then ran to my seat in the middle box on the right, the best acoustics in the house. When I got to my seat, I read the program over again, satisfied with the name we'd chosen for the first piece. When I finished reading and looked up, you were well into the first piece. I was sorry I'd missed so much. For a second I was afraid you'd forget something or make a mistake, but I needn't have worried; you always had all your concert work memorized perfectly and you knew your way around a keyboard perfectly. I watched your beautiful shoulders contract. I watched the way you snapped your head back at the end of the first piece. I saw the tiny points of gold on the bottom of your chin where the light caught your sweat. I felt the strength and stiffness of your thighs and calves when you pressed the pedals. I imagined the stiffness of your jaw and the way your teeth clenched when I had seen you practice at home. You were beautiful.

When it was over you stood up to bow. It was the best

I'd ever seen you do. Everyone clapped. I saw hundreds of pairs of hands clapping and people rising to applaud. I stood up and clapped furiously. I shouted, "Bravo! Bravo! Bravo!" I was beaming with pride and I kept shouting, "Bravo! Bravo!" You must have heard my voice because I saw you look for me. You turned your head toward every part of the auditorium trying to hear exactly where my voice was coming from. You looked like you were lost. I stopped shouting and ran down to get you. As I ran I noticed people glancing at me, then glancing away. I figured they probably knew I was yours, the one to whom the concert had been dedicated, as noted in the program. I went backstage to where I'd left you before the concert. You had just walked offstage. I grabbed you and held you. I felt the heat and moisture of your sweat through your clothes. Your muscles felt tight as they always did after a concert, but you sank into me as if you didn't have bones. Within minutes, friends and people from the Center came up to congratulate you. They patted you on the back and shook your hand. They did the same to me, smiling and talking. But there was too much at once and I couldn't see what anyone was saying; I wasn't used to reading anybody's lips but yours. You nodded and smiled graciously. You held onto my arm and thanked the voices. I nodded slightly and smiled. People shook my hand. Then I felt your fingers on my palm and I read, "Let's leave." You leaned close to me. I smelled your flesh and felt the heat of your face against mine. I put my arm around you and we left. I walked straight to where they had a limo waiting for you. You kept turning behind to say, "Thank you." As we got in the limo you told the driver to take us home, we weren't feeling up to the reception. I loved being with you and I loved your not wanting to be with all the other people who wanted to see you; I loved your needing me after you got offstage.

The driver closed the door behind us. The leather smelled like Windex. My hand felt squeaky against it. The limo pulled away. We could barely feel the movement. Everything was big and black and smooth and shiny. We held each other. Then you sat up and put your hands on my face.

"It was beautiful," I said.

You asked me something, but it was too dark to see your lips. Your fingers tapped my palm. "How do you know?"

"You were," I answered out loud. "You were beautiful." I leaned over to hold you but you pushed me back. I put my hand on your lips. I could see your face directed towards mine in the flashing lights from outside as we drove through the city. Your face was lit by blue, then white, then red, then yellow, the colors of neon signs over bars and store windows and movie marquees and stoplights. You didn't say anything for several minutes. I felt the moisture of your lips where my fingers were on your mouth.

"What?" I asked.

You pulled my other hand toward you and pressed the palm against your eye. I felt the hard solid marble underneath your skin. You leaned against me. I read your fingers. "You yelled 'Bravo'?"

"Of course it was me." I looked at your face changing

colors. "You mean you didn't know?"

"Not sure," you continued, "sound different. Never heard you shout."

You had been telling me for a while that my voice was changing. That was understandable, of course. I couldn't hear myself speak anymore, and I didn't speak much anyway. Hardly to anyone except you.

I wondered what I sounded like now. I had almost forgotten what I had sounded like before. But I didn't want to dwell on things or miss things. Besides, I had you. And what I didn't have, you did.

When we got home you called the hostess of the reception and told her you were too exhausted after your big return to party, but thanked her graciously. It was going to be just a short conversation, but you stayed on the phone a long time, unconsciously unbuttoning your shirt as you talked.

I watched your face as you undressed. I tried to read your lips but it was hard because the phone was over your mouth. But I saw your face light up. During the first part of the conversation you didn't say much. You just listened and smiled and said, "Oh, thanks, thanks," nodding. You always nodded your head slightly when you said this, and put your lips together. "Oh thanks, really." In the latter part of the conversation you started asking questions. You were sitting on the side of the bed and your right hand motioned in those little forward circles, the way you always did when you asked anything. You asked short questions then long ones prefaced by statements. You nodded slightly, uncon-

sciously, to the answers. Your whole face looked like pleasure and I thought that, now, your being unable to see
other peoples' faces, somehow made you forget anyone
could see yours. Your face hid nothing anymore. Your flesh
colored and shone. Your eyes were like cloudy steel balls.

When you got off the phone you stood up and faced me.
You were beaming.

"What was that all about?" I smiled to see you so happy.

"It was good. It was really, really good." Your right hand
was straight, the fingers together, chopping slightly in the
air towards me on "good" and "really."

"The conversation?"

Your head shook. "No, the concert. She said it was really
good."

"Sure it was. I told you it was. It was beautiful."

"Yeah, yeah . . ." you said quickly. You lifted your head
as if you were looking at something. You didn't know how
I was looking at you.

"Didn't I tell you it was beautiful? You heard me clapping
and yelling."

"Of course, baby," you said, more to pacify than to agree
with me. You put your hand toward me. I took it and guid-
ed it to my stomach. I was lying down, you were leaning up
on your side facing me. "Of course, baby, you loved it."

I reached up to your cheek.

"Not the acoustics, not the piano. She said it was me —
my work."

I wondered what you were looking at. Your skin shone
with warmth. My hand slid down your cheek, cupping

your chin, then down your neck.

You leaned over me to flip off the light by the bed, but I grabbed your hand and put it on my ribs, pulling you down against me.

"I have to see you," I said.

This was the first time we had done it since we'd done it.

Your body eased up next to me. It was warm against my skin. Your left hand moved over my ribs. You had told me how you liked the leanness of my body, the way the ribs were hard and near the surface of my skin, and the spaces between them soft and giving. I ran my hand up your spine slowly, then onto your shoulders. You put your head on my neck. I felt the movement of your stomach and chest as you breathed. I looked up through your hair to the overhead light. Its two bulbs were hidden by a square, curved, milky-white shade. I saw the small black dots of dead bugs dropped in the shade, the plastic white button that screwed the shade to the fixture. I felt a film of moisture on the small of your back.

That time you were quicker. I'd never noticed the way your skin changed color from your neck up. Your face got pink, then apricot. Your lips read out my name over and over. You put your lips together then dropped them, blowing out. Your tongue fell behind your bottom teeth. Then you inhaled with your mouth and I watched you say my name again and again, faster, until you didn't say it anymore. Your eyelids shook. Then you sank like a rag. Your mouth was open. Your whole body was pink. I looked up at the ceiling. The light was still on. You hadn't seen anything and nothing had happened to me.

Our second excursion out, we went to the travelling exhibit of Turner's work. We walked close, our arms around each others' backs. I read the guide notes and described the paintings. Your fingers asked questions on my arm or hand.

We stopped in front of the first painting.

"You know, his later stuff is so different. You can see where he comes from, like that sky, but . . ."

You squeezed my arm. Your fingers tapped, "What?"

This was the first time I'd had to describe something new to you, something important. Everything else was around our house; you remembered.

"Well, the light is nice, the canvas is sort of cluttered . . ."

You pinched me, then tapped my hand, "Picture?"

"Oh, boats, ships, I mean, and people . . ." I stuttered.

You squeezed my hand. I hadn't spoken loudly enough. This had been a problem with me lately. I said again, "Ships and people."

You pulled my hand. "Title."

I leaned forward to read the card at the side of the painting. I turned you to face the painting as if you could see it. I whispered, "It's called "The Battle of Trafalgar as seen from the Mizen Starboard Shroud of the Victory, 1806–1808'."

I paused. I didn't know what to say. "Well, it's got lots of ships, a dozen or so, and a dock going out. Some people on the dock, a priest kneeling down, not really kneeling though, and six or eight soldiers, red uniforms with white stripes across their chests, a guy with a George Washington hat, and a bunch of yellow steam, gold really, morning light, and stays hanging down."

I stopped talking and just looked at it, then stepped back, pulling you with me, to see how it looked from three feet away.

"I didn't even notice that from up close."

You tugged my arm quickly, then released it, "What?"

I whispered, "Some of those stays go exactly like this." I dropped your hand to make a pyramid shape with my arms, but you snatched my arm back before I could gesture. I was surprised because always before, whenever you were afraid and needed to grab me, I would know it first. You would gasp a little and I would hold you before your fear had a chance to set in.

"What?"

You grabbed my palm and tapped frantically while you whispered in my ear. But I was so distracted by your mouth next to my ear that I couldn't understand your fingers on my hand. I clasped your hand and moved my head away from yours.

"Don't let go of me." Your teeth and lips were tight. I could barely read you.

"I'm sorry, I just wanted to — "

Your fingers scratched my palm: "Don't let go."

I looked at you. Your eyes were looking somewhere behind me.

When we got to the next painting, I was thrilled. I inhaled through my teeth.

You tugged my arm again.

"Sorry. "Hannibal Crossing the Alps." You know."

You shook your head.

"Come on, of course you do. It's really famous. You'd recognize it."

You slapped my stomach.

"OK," I sighed, "it's black and orange. The sky going crazy and you — you just have to feel it." I couldn't imagine what you imagined this painting would look like.

That night in bed you leaned over me to turn out the light, the way you always did before, but hadn't since that first night after the concert when I asked you to leave it on because I needed to see you clearly and not be in the dark. I said, "What are you doing? Please don't."

You were up on your elbow, one arm stretched over me towards the light. Your face was straight at me. You smiled as if to comfort me. Your lips moved, "It's OK, baby, it's OK." Then it was dark and your palms were on my cheeks. You were lying down, pulling me down, too. I couldn't hear or see anything. You pulled my right hand under your neck and up over your face. You put it on your mouth. I felt your lips move and the warmth and moisture of air coming out of your mouth; you were talking. You put my left hand on your stomach. I felt the smooth skin of your stomach and your stomach muscles tightening under my hand. I felt the loose skin on the back of your hand and the soft line of hair that ran from your chest to your crotch and the stiff curly hair of your crotch. You pressed my hand to your moving lips, talking. I touched your neck. I could tell you were speaking aloud.

"What are you saying?" I tried to imagine what your lips looked like.

I started up, but you pulled me down and rolled on top of me. You lay over me, putting your mouth by my ear. Your lips were moving near my ear and your tongue and breath, but I couldn't hear anything. I imagined the sound of your voice saying my name out loud over and over and the sound the air made as you pulled it down into your throat with your mouth open when you came, which was the same sound as the last sound I heard, the gasp you gasped as I pushed out your eyes.

We're standing in the kitchen, arm's distance apart, facing each other. I have two shiny silver teaspoons, and you, the two wood-burning pens we'd found in your old toy box at home. We raise our tools to face level. Your eyes are the color of sky. The light, cool spoons are against your cheeks. I hear the soft muffled rustle of your hands against my hair, the swish of your palms against my cheeks, the hum of the electric burning pens. I keep my eyes open, then press the round cold spoons into your eye sockets, push the sides of them in, perpendicular to your face. You try to blink; I press them back. My head feels like coals. I can feel everything. I clench my eyes closed. Everything is hot again. You gasp.

You gasped. I jolted up, screaming. I felt the movement in my throat and vibrations in my head and I couldn't hear anything. You fell away from me but reached back to put your arms around me, your hand over my mouth. You sat up and held me.

I fumbled for the light and switched it on. When I looked at you, your eyes were wide open. Your lips were saying, "It's OK, it's OK, it's OK."

We kept the light on the rest of the night and every night after that.

You learned Braille and I learned ASL. But we still didn't want anyone to know. I borrowed Braille books from the library and made it obvious to everyone I could see. One day, on a bus on the way home from the library, we sat across from a boy with a hearing aid. I watched him as unobtrusively as I could. We sat next to each other, your hand on my arm, and I didn't tell you. I watched his face to see if I could tell how much he could hear. He was travelling by himself. I sent off to the American Sign Language Association for information about teaching the deaf to speak. We had agreed to tell no one, but I knew you were becoming increasingly annoyed at my inability to control my voice. And I wanted to do something about it on my own. Besides, there was no way you could find out; I was in charge of the mail.

But when I got the information I realized I was more interested in the articles about operations and treatments that cured some kinds of deafness. I read that in some cases there was scar tissue that could be removed. I tried to figure out a way of going to see an ear specialist and leaving you alone. I thought about it for weeks.

You wrote me a note saying that the change in my voice was drastic. You wrote that it was not just a matter of tone or pitch anymore, it was my ability to form words, that sometimes I yelled and sometimes you could barely hear me, that I didn't speak clearly and I needed to work on my enunciation. You wrote that maybe I'd better cool it on talking until I could talk better.

Your note was sloppily written. The characters bumped into each other, the lines were crooked. Some of the words weren't even written completely on the page.

Our first big social occasion was the costume party. We even skipped the reception after my show at the Meyer Gallery. We went because we thought it would be safe because, if anything went wrong, we could plead drunk or "in character." And, of course, we could always play up the "reclusive artist ill-at-ease in social situations" role. We went as two medieval saints: hair shirts, stigmati, crowns of thorns, the works. Any social shortcomings caused by our handicaps could be excused as part of our costumes.

It was a huge party and everyone was there. I recognized some people by height and build, or if their costume was simple; you recognized their voice. But everyone was wearing masks and I couldn't see anyone's lips. Sometimes people came up and shook my hand or kissed me or gave me a pat on the back. I wanted to know what they were saying. I kept asking you, tapping your hand or whispering, "What are they saying? What's going on?" But you didn't want me to interrupt your conversations.

Every time I leaned over to ask you or tap out some-thing, I saw people chuckle and nudge each other. A courtier pinched me on the arm and winked, then mim-icked our constant closeness by putting both arms around the troubador nearby and whispering. Later, I gave up talk-ing with any of the faces I couldn't see.

You and I were sitting on a couch; you were talking to two people to our right, and had been for forty minutes. My hand was on your knee. You were gesturing wildly. I felt your body shake as you laughed. You slapped your hand down on mine, grabbed it tightly, then released it. Your hands went in the air again and you weren't touching me. I thought about how familiar and common our bodies were with one another; your slapping my hand when you laughed was as natural as slapping your own thigh, as if there was no difference between them.

Then a skeleton yanked me away from the couch and pulled me out to the dance floor. I think you must have shouted after my being pulled away from you: it felt like the slow, hard pull between two magnets, then the snap of release. I positioned myself facing you. You were shaking your head frantically right and left. You must have been shouting because the couple next to you put their arms around you to comfort you. I imagined them telling you to settle down, that it was OK, that of course I wasn't upset with you.

They looked at me and back at you, trying to figure us out. I waved and smiled, indicating there was nothing really wrong, that you were just the way you were sometimes, high strung.

I tried to catch the rhythm of the dance from watching everyone else move. But I didn't know if I was moving on the beat or on the half-beat. I hoped the music was loud enough so my partner wouldn't try to talk to me. I felt the rhythm on the floor. I felt my blood go faster inside my temples and the moisture warming inside my clothes.

When the dance was over I came back and sat down. You threw your arms around me and put your head under my chin and on my shoulder. You were trying to cry. I felt the warmth and wetness of the sweat and saliva through my costume. I felt the trembling of your body. I lifted your face up. Your eyes were closed. Your face was red but you couldn't cry. I thought how you must have felt, trying to cry but not being able to, like trying to vomit and all you could do was the dry heaves. Your stomach was moving, short and quick. You were gasping. You were holding my hand with both of yours. You were squeezing it, "Home — home — home — "

We both smelled like cigarettes and sweat, but neither of us showered before we went to bed. You lay there shaking without crying. I imagined the sound of your sobbing. I wanted to say something, that I was sorry: for the dance, for the party, for everything, for what we'd done. But I didn't. I didn't open my mouth because I knew I couldn't talk clearly anymore. And that, though you would probably understand me, the sound of my voice was horrible to you. I wanted to tap out "I'm sorry" on your skin. I put my hand on your naked stomach. I started to raise and lower my fingers, but I stopped. I hated talking this way, the only way we could communicate in the same way; I hated it because it was the only way.

I didn't tap out the words "I'm sorry" because I didn't know what they meant. And because I didn't really mean that. But I had to take the risk that you would know what I meant. That what I meant by not using our only way of communicating, our little, secret way, was that I wanted us to have a new one. That this new way was how I would tell you I would never leave you. Ever, even for an instant out in the world. That we would stay and watch out for each other.

That was what I meant when I flattened my palm out straight and still on your stomach and put my head on your chest to sleep.

But I don't know if you knew what I meant; you were almost still; your sobbing had stopped. I think we slept.

So we didn't go out again. We stayed inside with one another. During the day you composed and I painted. At night we read or I watched TV and you listened to the radio in our room. It was nice because we fit each other like glove and hand. If I wanted to go to sleep early but you wanted to listen to the radio, the noise didn't bother me. I could fall asleep in your arms while you listened to the *1812 Overture*. Or if you wanted to sleep and I wanted to watch TV, I could keep it on and the flickering of the screen wouldn't bother you.

Our house was warm and peaceful. We shared everything. What was yours was mine; what was mine was yours. We had no ambitions and no fear.

One night I wanted to stay up and do some studies for my new piece, *Voices*. It was a huge red-orange fiery roundish globe with lines of blue and white curling over it. It was an abstract piece about the sound the air made when you pulled it down into your throat with your mouth open.

I was very taken with my work then. Sometimes I would stay up working very late. My canvases had grown huge. My work was very physical and massive. I knew I must have made lots of noise, so I worked downstairs where you couldn't hear me.

That night I worked till three. When I started upstairs to our room, something smelled wrong. As I reached the landing I saw the light in our room was off. I wondered if it had burnt out because we always kept it on for me. You would never have turned it off. But when I reached the top of the stairs I saw into our room.

You were sprawled on the bed in a pool of blood. Your neck and stomach and crotch and hands and face and mouth were red. The sheets were red. I didn't know you had so much blood. And there kept on being more.

Then I heard the sound of the running blood and I heard the sound inside myself of mine. Inside of me it sounded like snow, like I was driving into a tunnel under snow. I hadn't heard like that before. It was the first thing I had heard since we had done it.

I walked to the bed and sat on the bed and sat beside

your body and picked up the phone. I couldn't hear the dial tone but I dialed 911. I couldn't hear when they picked up the phone or if or when they answered, and I didn't know and I couldn't tell, if whoever it was could understand what I was trying to say. So I kept saying over again, "Hello? Hello? Something's happened — Hello? There's something wrong — Hello? There's someone stabbed — I didn't hear — I couldn't hear — Hello?"

I stayed on the phone and repeated this over and over because I didn't know when someone would answer, or how long it would take to understand, or if somebody ever would, or why I couldn't say right what had happened, why I couldn't tell what we'd done.

LOVE POEM

It's like art, making and unmaking. You're attracted to misshapen blocks. You like to chisel and form them into something beautiful and show yourself that you can do it. And you can do it. You do it beautifully. Why, look at all the things you've made beautiful. You've had shows in internationally renowned galleries. Everyone loves your work. Everyone says what a miracle worker you are, and you are. Here are some of your works: *Lazarus, The Woman Who Died, Spring in December, A Sunny Day in Chicago in November, Piña Colada in Salt Lake City, Love Among the Ruins, Blood From Stone, A Fine Shoot of Green in the Arctic, Love Among the Ruins II, Love Among the Ruins III.*

You're acclaimed. Everyone clamors about you. Everyone loves you.

But they don't know your secret.

One night after your opening at the Tate last September — the Queen came, the Prime Minister came, David Bowie came, John Lennon came, Peter Cook and Dudley Moore came — one night after your opening, someone broke into the gallery and tore apart all your beautiful canvases. Someone soldered down all your beautiful metal sculpture. They broke your marbles. They smashed your glass. They burnt your wood. (You work in many mediums.)

The next day, the papers were full of it and the *Times* and the *Guardian* interviewed you. There were correspondents from New York, Washington, L.A., Chicago. They interviewed you about the destruction of your beautiful work and took pictures of you crying over the destruction of your beautiful work. But you wouldn't let them take many pictures or ask many questions because, as you and your agent told them repeatedly, you were much too distraught about the destruction of your beautiful work. How could anyone want to, you asked. Everyone asked: how could anyone want to? Everyone shook their heads. Such beautiful work — irreplaceable. Your picture on the front page of the *Times* was poignant and moving. I could barely see your face (your head was turned from the camera), but I could see your tears. I saw your tears and they looked real even to me. They streaked down your face gorgeously, like one of your drip paintings after Helen Frankenthaller. Yes, you were very beautiful.

I had the paper sent up to my room where I was staying at the Y near Russell Square. I'd paid the paper boy the day before because I knew you'd be in the paper.

I knew because you and I had done it. We'd done it for old times' sake. We'd had a few quick ones at the Prince of Wales, and then we'd done it. We did it to finish off something we'd left undone. I did it because I wanted to. You did it because you wanted to, too, because I told you I was the only person who knew you wanted to, and because I was the only person who would tell you that, and because I was the only person who would help you do it. You also did it for the insurance.

We let ourselves into the Tate with your master key, which had been entrusted to you by the Tate Gallery Trustees. I took chains and knives and razors and a whip and a machine gun and a sword and a cat-o'-nine-tails and three hand grenades and a liter of sulphuric acid and a power drill with four big drill bits. You didn't take anything because you wanted to do it with your own bare hands. The only thing you carried was a flashlight.

We went in and didn't turn on any of the lights. We did that for old times' sake, too. We went through your exhibition and destroyed everything. I slashed and shot and blowtorched and cut and soldered and blasted and whipped and drilled. You hit and kicked and tore and bit and clawed. Some pieces we did separately and some pieces we did under the soft grey glow of your flashlight. We worked almost the whole night and made rubble of everything.

But then I asked you if we could turn the lights on, please, because suddenly my old fear of the dark was on me again, and I was afraid. But you said we couldn't because you couldn't see anything because you had to look surprised when the sympathetic police and curators brought you here tomorrow to see what horrid vandalism had occurred the night before. I said I understood, and I closed my eyes to pretend it was only dark because I had my eyes closed and that it was really light. And then I asked you to tell me it was light and you said, but it wasn't, and I said, did you think I was a fool, of course I knew it was dark, but I just wanted to be told it wasn't, and you didn't understand, but I said, Lie to me, dammit, lie to me, so you did.

You took me in your arms and you said, It's light, it's light, it's light, it's light, and you held me and told me that it was light through the rest of the night until just before morning, and then we had to leave before the gallery opened. You led me to the exit door by the hand (my eyes were still closed), and outside where it was beginning to be light, and you told me to open my eyes, that it was beginning to get light. I did and then we shook hands on the steps of the gallery and patted each other on the shoulders like comrades and vowed secrecy. Then we each went home. You took a cab to Grosvenor Square and I hurried to the Russell Square Station Y. I went to bed for a few minutes and dreamt. This is what I dreamt:

I dreamt that I became an artist, too, and what I did was make and destroy things just like you. But no matter what I did, either in making or destroying it, no one cared. They didn't consider me an artist or a criminal. They didn't say, what a shame. They never gave me coverage. They never noticed me and I didn't know why, because, after all, I was just doing exactly what you had done and, not only that, what I had taught you to do and what you and I had done together.

I woke up when the paper boy brought me the paper with your picture and the articles about your show. I thought how I was the only person in the world who knew the real story. I knew that you knew it too, but I also knew that you would never think about it, that you would forget it.

I will not forget it. I will tell it to myself again and again and again.

THE DEATH OF NAPOLEON: ITS INFLUENCE ON HISTORY

I think about him all the time. I make up stories about him and dream about him. In fact, that's not really accurate. The dreams aren't so much about him as they are about his death and me killing him. I don't know very much about him. All I know is that I have to kill him and that I think about him all the time and the ways that I can kill him and exactly how I will do it.

I thought of him tonight at the Daniels' and today at work on the subway to and from work and on the way to and from the Daniels' while we were talking and I didn't tell you. You didn't know what I was thinking about at all. We were talking about your sister and you didn't know I was thinking about him.

He's going to be on "Meet the Press." The studio is all lit up and the lights are blaring, silver and bright everywhere. It smells like sweat and makeup. Edwin Newman is there and someone is straightening his tie and coat as he's looking at some notes in a manila folder. I notice that he's much better looking in person than on TV. I'm working on one of the cameras when I see him come out. He's short and he has on white pants, a dark coat with tails, and a red vest. His hair is slicked down, black, and he's got on a tricorn hat. He's standing about four feet away from me when I throw an extension cord at him that's in the shape of a lasso just as I'm snipping the end with a pair of heavy cutting shears. When it hits him, he turns into a red-orange glowing doughboy, like a Christmas ornament. He hops in the air, twisting and flopping. Everything is very sudden. It smells of burnt flesh and makeup and I've got him.

You and I are having a talk. We're talking about plans and goals and you've mentioned the probability of your going back to school for your masters if the promotion doesn't come through. You aren't, however, going to rule out the possibility of something totally unexpected like, for example, moving up to Vermont for a while with Bob and Debra if they were really serious and if we could get into living on a farm. You say that, mostly, you just want to be true to yourself and not fix yourself into anything that's not really you. Also, you want to consider me and do what's best for both of us. Then you ask me what I think is important for me and what I want to do and I tell you:

"I want to kill Napoleon."

"You what?"

"I want to kill Napoleon."

"What do you mean?"

"I mean I want to kill him."

"C'mon, what is this?"

"I want to kill Napoleon."

"OK, OK, I give. What's the punch line?"

"There isn't one. I just want to kill him."

Then you look at me and you say, "Right." Then you ask, "How come?" and I say, "I have to," and you say, "You don't have to." You say, "He's dead. He's been dead for a hundred and fifty years." You say, "What is this?" And you look at me.

You look at me and you wonder what's got into me. You wonder if you're dealing with me in the best way. You look kind and sympathetic. I look at you. Both of us are proud to look the other straight in the eye. It's something we've built up. You ask me why. I look straight at you and ask you, "Have you ever wanted to kill Napoleon?" and you say, "No," and I say, "Oh." Then I say, "Well, I do. I want to kill him. I mean, I have to kill him." You ask me why, and I tell you I don't know.

They're doing a remake of *King Kong* in Hollywood.

They hire Napoleon as the woman abducted from the sky-scraper and me as Kong. In the famous scene, I'm careful to remove him gingerly from the skyscraper. When I bring him to my face, I hardly recognize him. He looks like a cake decoration, only not so powdery; he's immaculate. I press my fingers to my palm, then fold my thumb over in a very tight fist. When I unclench my hand and ease my fingers open, I think of a Mamma Bellosi Delux Supreme With Everything. To go.

I spend a whole evening thinking of him. At home you ask me what I thought of the movie. I say I think some of it was really good, but I wasn't really concentrating on it. You ask me why and I tell you that I was thinking of Napoleon and you look at me. I was thinking how crippled I feel at not being able to abbreviate his name or call him by a nick-name or a pet name. Any abbreviation or derivation sounds ridiculous. But then I reason that that is part of who he is; he is inextricably Napoleon. Nothing abbreviated or trans-latable, and I must kill him.

Tonight we're doing dishes after dinner. The Daniels have been over. We've played bridge and eaten lots. I am wash-ing. You are drying and putting them away. You use a soft linen dishcloth and I use a plastic aqua-colored ball. My hands are getting pruny and my fingernails are white and soft. The water is greenish-grey with pieces of spaghetti noodles. Orange dots of grease are in it. We talk about the evening with the Daniels. We're just about finished. I've

washed everything except the silverware. I pick up a hand-
ful of it. I lift it out of the water. It shines and feels slick in
my hand. I dunk it back under and almost release my hand
to let the pieces separate so I can scrub them individually,
but then it's his puffy white neck in my hand. I look in the
water and see his white, greenish face. His cheeks are bloat-
ed and he looks like panic. I tighten my hold and look. His
hair loosens from being perfectly, tightly combed. It sways
like seaweed or a mermaid's hair. His flesh is soft between
my fingers and I tighten my grip, afraid he will be able to
slip out because the water is greasy from the meatballs. His
face is colored like a fish's stomach and I think how when
fish drown they float up on their stomachs and their white
stomachs surface like his puffy fleshy face. His lips pale into
the color of peach melba yogurt. His hair sways like a mermaid's. I've never realized how long it was because it has
always been stuck down. The water starts looking vaguely
pink and I think that that must be from his red sash. I imagine his body being squeezed up through the drain and how
it must curve like an "S" coming up through the pipe.
When I feel him start to struggle, I hold even tighter, until
there is only a little resistance, and release him.

Then I turn on the disposal.

We're at a museum, looking at a show of lesser known
contemporary artists. Hardly any of the work is representa-
tional. We talk about the work and you ask me what I think
of a certain piece.

"What do you see in it?"

"Well, I don't know. Nothing really."

"It must evoke something, make you feel something."

"Yeah . . ."

"Well, what does it make you think of?"

"It reminds me of Napoleon."

"Napoleon? How come?"

"It just does."

"I don't see it at all."

"I guess I don't either. It just reminds me of him."

"Everything reminds you of Napoleon."

"Yeah. I guess so."

I think about him all the time.

I'm at the Coronation. I'm standing next to David, helping him squeeze oil out and mix it on the palette. We're about twenty yards away from him and I can smell excitement and bodies behind our corner of oil and turpentine. David is nice to me. He chats with me in French and I start to tell him that I've only studied two and a half years of high school French and that I can't remember any of it, but then I realize that I'm telling him this in perfect fluent French, and halt in mid-sentence. Fortunately he hasn't been listening and I am not a fool. He has long, thin, creamy-colored fingers, smooth-skinned hands with fine delicate lines. He is very neat and ordered. He sets the blops of paint where he wants them, equidistant from each other on the palette. I want to ask him how he can be so confident and just paint it like this, but then I notice a huge sheaf of pencil sketches and studies for this and wonder how he did them because this is the Coronation and it's never happened before. There's lots of music and noise. Glasses clink and it's more like a party than a coronation. Everyone mingles and chats. Then someone says, "OK, OK, everybody, places," and everyone gets in place. He's standing on a platform in the front and starts giving a speech in a French I can't understand. David turns to me, palm turned upright, and like a doctor saying "Suture," says, "Number nine, light." I go to hand him a palette knife but pick up a violin case instead. The lid falls open as I lift it up and out falls a sawn-off machine gun. I catch it before it hits the ground and rat-a-tat off three clips of shells at him and the rest of them, everyone except myself and David. Everyone looks red.

"We've really gotten close lately. I don't know, I just feel so good about things. I've been feeling really good lately."

"Yeah?"

"Uh huh. We have a lot more in common all the time. I really realize it more and more."

"Yeah . . ."

"I feel, like, there's more things you understand about me and I do about you that we don't even have to say."

"Yeah, really."

"Do you feel that way?"

"Sure."

"Like, I really know what you're thinking when you don't even say it."

"Yeah, really."

November. I am walking up a hill near Painswick in the Stroud valley, Gloucestershire, England. Everything is brown and grey and wet. I'm wearing dark brown shoes, slightly scuffed, with dark brown laces. The tips of the laces are the color of toffee. The path is dipped and holed from where the rain goes down. The ground is slippery and I walk cautiously. My hands, gloved and stuffed into my coat pockets, are cold. My face feels cold and hot and I know I will be red when I go back in. My glasses will fog over and I'll barely be able to see myself in the mirror when I take off my coat in the entrance hall.

I'm climbing up a hill. Behind me and below, the path twists down into Sheepscombe. Grey smoke goes up from the chimneys. I go up, and my thighs and calves hurt. I stand up to catch my breath. When I look up, I see him.

He is standing on a plateau, elevated about two feet above the top of the hill. I wonder if he's cold from exposure. I think that anyone else's boots would be smeared from the climb, but I know his aren't and I wish the sun was there to catch the glint off them. His strong head is pressed into his coat. His fine red sash is like Christmas candy, brilliant like eye-blood, straight across his stomach. He stands straight and doesn't look as if he feels the cold. He wears nothing on his hands.

He's looking straight ahead, past me, to my right. I turn around to see if I can see what he's looking at, but all I can see is the furry line between the woods and sky, and parts of smoke in tails, rising. I turn back toward him and stop. I breathe in deeply, press my hands into my pockets more and start to walk again. My toes are cold and my cold feet feel hard stones pressing on the soles. I go up slowly. He's about fifty feet away.

The path is steeper. I can't imagine him walking up here and I wonder how he got here. I walk up and feel cold go in my lungs. He stays still, looking at the fuzzy line of horizon behind me. I know that I can't see the things he can in the fuzzed horizon, or past it, and I know that this is why I love him. I feel good, having to work at the climb and I like the greyness of my breath, quickening and heavier as I try harder on the steeper path to approach him. I take my hands from my pockets, remove my gloves, and walk with my cold sweaty hands exposed.

I'm closer to him now, within shouting distance, and I want to say something. I think he must see me or know I am coming. I don't expect him to say anything and I want to say something.

I'm only twenty feet away from him. I keep climbing and I can see his boots clearly and there is no mud on them. I can see the thick seams on the sides of his tight white legs, the wrinkles over his kneecaps. I can see the rise of his shoulders as he breathes. Now I can see his clear heavy eyes fixed on the line behind me. I want to turn around again, but I don't. I keep looking at him. His wrist is red between his sleeve and the opening in his jacket. His other hand is red as well. His face is still and I am close enough to know he hears me stop and breathe. Five feet from him, I stop and look. I want to say hello and then he starts to turn to me. He's facing me, direct on, and then he starts to turn away. He lifts his right foot slightly and puts it behind himself to turn. His right thigh tightens, and his calf, pulling him around. His left hip, where his white tights and jacket meet, turns towards me. He puts his right foot on the ground and shifts his weight to that. Then he lifts his left foot forward. His eyes lower and he moves his left foot in front of himself.

Suddenly I feel desperate and I want to say his name out loud. I want to call him, "Napoleon! Napoleon!" He turns from me on a circle; the part that turns away from me goes into air. He's walking into air. I say, "Napoleon — " but I can't say it out loud. Now his back is to me, but only half of his back, the right half has disappeared. He's turned into the air. "Napoleon — " His left foot lifts again, forward, to its right; he turns. The left tail of his coat catches on air and his shoulder looks like a cliff. His hair is black and solid, shiny. His boot is smooth. The spur is silver. "Napoleon — " He lifts his foot. The spur goes up like a stone. I hear the crunch of rock beneath his moving foot. His foot is forward and right. The line moves over my vision like a card cutting over a lens. "Napoleon — " He puts his foot down. The instant it would touch, he's gone. I lunge forward, throwing myself at his boot. My hand slaps on a smooth large stone.

"Napoleon! Napoleon!"
Your hands.
"Napoleon — I love you. Napoleon — "
Everything is dark. Your hands are on me.
"Wake up. It's OK. You're just dreaming. I'm here.

You're just dreaming."

I hear myself breathe and feel your hands trying to calm my body and I feel water going in my chest.

"It's only a nightmare. I'm here. Are you OK?"

"Yeah, yeah. I'm OK. Did you hear what I said?"

"I couldn't make it out, but you were screaming something. Do you remember?"

I hesitate, not looking at you. "No . . ."

He and I are standing in a train station. One of us is here to see the other one off, but I'm not sure which is which. It's cold and I only have on a sweater. He is bareheaded and his right arm is stuck inside his jacket. I feel very close with him and believe he feels so for me as well. We've just walked through the turnstile and are walking toward the track. We are silent.

I feel cold wind drifting through the station from where the trains will come in. It's a completely covered station and I can see yellow lines of light curving in as the trains come. There are several tracks. We are waiting by the first one. I feel very tender and know we will be parting in a minute.

He turns and looks up at me. "I have something for you." He speaks English with a French accent, low and woolly. He's wanting to be secretive. "It's only a little something, but I want you to have it." He pulls a coin out of his left side pocket, holds out his open palm to me, and I see a small bronze coin. "For you." He holds it out to me and I take it. "It belonged to my mother." He looks into the distance. "My mother, she was a saint." He holds the moment, then looks at me. "I want you to have it." I look down at the coin as he presses it into my palm. "Oh, Napoleon," I say very softly, gazing at the bronze dot in my palm. I raise my eyes to look at him tenderly. Then I step forward to embrace him.

He snaps back, hissing through his teeth. "Not here — anyone could see us!" His eyes flash. I know he's embarrassed about being two heads shorter than I am, and do not pursue my embrace. I look at him with apology in my eyes and he turns away to face the track where the train will arrive. He puts his hand behind his back as if both hands were behind his back, clasped and relaxed, but the other hand is in his jacket. I think how painful it must be to be so proud, and I know that he knows I understand this. I look at his firm straight back, the way his shiny heels touch each other, the firm lines of his thighs beneath his coattails. His shoulders are thrown back. We wait several minutes for the train, then see two yellow lines start across the opposite wall. The train is arriving and we move closer to the track to board. I can just see the circles of light and hear the train turning in a direct approach to the track. As the lines of light straighten and the train approaches, I remember which one of us has the ticket. When the train is about twenty feet away, I toss the coin in front of it. He spins around to ask me what I'm doing and I push him on to the track.

You tell me I've been sleeping badly lately and I say why, and you say I turn in my sleep and I often wake up sweating and clenching the sheets tight in my fist. I tell you I've been dreaming about Napoleon and killing him and you ask who and I say, "Napoleon," and you say, "No, I know it's Napoleon, but who is it really?" and I say, "What do you mean?" and you say you don't think it's just Napoleon.

You say, "It's not Napoleon you're trying to kill. It's a real person. You're trying to kill a real person," and I say, "I hadn't thought of it that way," and I hadn't.

I'm standing outside the Great Hall. It's a special day called the Hearing of Complaints and lots of people are here to petition him. Most of the people are men in old military uniforms. I'm one of the only civilians. The guard opens the door and I hear my name. He ushers me into this huge hall with tons of people standing along the sides. He's at the far end, dressed in a furry leopard robe over his standard dress. The guard holds a silver platter out to me and I put the index card with my complaints on it. Then he gives me the plate and I walk forward to the throne and him. When I get there, someone stops me and tells me to read my case. I give a long speech with words like "whereas," "heretofore," "party of the first part," and "breach of trust." Then I get to the "acquired debts requesting payment." I look up at him before I start reading. He looks uninterested. I know the other people have been petitioning for lands in Alsace-Lorraine, or the freedom of their Prussian village, or the repayment of their country estates.

I look down at my blue-lined index card on the silver tray and read:

You owe me thirty-one dollars.

You still haven't returned my favorite aqua flannel night-shirt or my blue bandanna.

You owe me two Italian dinners, one movie, and a ride to Nashville.

You owe me an incalculable number of breakfasts in bed.

You haven't returned my St. Francis medal or my Buffalo Springfield *Retrospective* album.

You owe me half of the *New Yorkers* we subscribed to and every other month's worth of the Book-of-the-Month-Club selection.

When I look up at him, he looks bored. He turns to one of the attendants next to him and asks him something I can't hear. The attendant looks at me and asks, "Is that all?" I want to say something else, but I don't. I just nod and play it cool. Then the attendant next to him says. "We'll keep your request on file for further consideration." Another attendant comes and takes the card off the plate and turns me around so I can leave. When he turns me, though, I move quicker than him. I spin back around and Frisbee the solid-silver platter right through his leopard robe. The edges sharpen as it spins through the air and I can hear the sing of air over the sharp edge. It spins into him like a turning saw-mill and it hits him in the stomach like a knife in an uncooked biscuit, and I'm spinning and every time I spin I have another plate in my hand and I throw it at him and it hits another place: across his face, his pudgy white thighs, the top of his slick black head. I keep going around and around and finding sharp silver Frisbees and I keep throwing them at him and they stick out of him like crooked red Venetian blinds.

I start telling you about my dreams. At first I'm embarrassed and wonder if you don't want to hear them, but you tell me that you do want to hear them. You care about them and you find them interesting, too, and so I tell you and you say, "I think Napoleon is Jerry." You say you recognize the coin, the hill, the debts. I can't believe it, but then I do. Then you ask me about Jerry and if he was anything like Napoleon, if he was short or spoke French or anything, and I say no. Then you ask me what it was like with him and I say I don't remember.

"Did you trust him?"

"I don't know."

"What do you mean?"

"Well, sort of."

You look at me and say, "Look, either you trust someone or you don't. It's not a matter of degree," and I say I don't remember.

We've spoken about Jerry before and you always ask me more than I want to tell, and it's good for me, but sometimes it goes too fast and I say, "I just don't remember what was real and what I'm making up."

And I wonder why I'm suddenly thinking of Jerry again because I haven't for a long time, and what suddenly reminded me of him? You didn't even know he was part of my history for a long time. Then I think about you saying that about trust, and the reason I couldn't tell you or didn't know is, if you do trust someone or think you do and then stop, does that mean you never really did? Also it means, how can you be sure if you thought you did, but then something happens and you think that maybe you didn't or shouldn't have.

I'm writing on a parchment with a long, old-fashioned, pointy-tipped pen. It says, "I thought this would hurt you most." It's a suicide note and I put it in my lap. I'm sitting in a boat without oars or a motor. I'm wearing a long heavy brocade dress and my fingers look skinny and white. I push off from the bank and float down the Seine to the palace. I know he's having a fête today and by the time I get to the palace, I'm dead. I'm dead but, since this is a dream, I can still see and feel everything, but from above and outside my body, like the movies. The boat catches in some bushes and people run down to see what's happened. They see a beautiful maiden with a long brocade dress, dead, in a boat. That's me. Then he struts up in his fine black boots. He walks on wet grass and mud by the river, but his boots remain immaculate. The sky is blue and everything is lovely. He has a glass of champagne in his hand. He approaches the boat. One of his attendants picks up the note and hands it to him. He gives the attendant his glass of champagne and reads the note. He rolls up his eyes, purses his lips, and shakes his head. He doesn't say anything but drops the note on the ground and turns back to the party.

This scene repeats itself over and over. Like trying to dial a phone number or start a car in a dream, you just can't do it, he won't respond at all. In the last repetition, though, there is a change. In this one, after he drops the note and turns away, I get out of the boat like a ghost and stab him in the back of the neck repeatedly with my pen. He dies slowly of blood loss and ink poisoning. His coat is all stained with red and blue. Then I get back into the boat and sit in the bushes.

I'm reading a book on Napoleon and you say that you wish I could get off this obsession, that it's not healthy for me, and I say you're probably right. You ask me about Jerry again and what happened and I say either, I don't remember, or, I don't want to think about it. You say you're glad you never met Jerry and you hope you never do because he sounds horrible and you wish I'd never met him either, and I don't know how I feel about that because I think maybe I did trust him and I wonder how he is.

We're playing bridge at the Daniels'. Mark and Sue are partners and my partner is him. He sits across from me at the shaky card table with the plastic canvas-looking top and deals the cards. He only uses one hand because his other one is stuck inside his coat. His pouchy, white stomach rubs against the side of the table. The Daniels have gone into the kitchen to get us all more beer and potato chips for the next rubber. I watch him deal and say, "It would be lots easier if you used both hands." He flashes his eyes at me. "It's only me," I say gingerly, "go ahead." I pause. "Take it out." He says, "I can do it with only one," in French. Then he smiles. I think he's teasing me and I get up to go around behind him, watching him deal. I stand over him and he starts humming the French national anthem. I'm sure he's joking with me and I reach over his shoulder to pull his arm out.

He cries out and drops the cards as the arm comes out with a pop. Instantly, there's a huge blast and his body is shot off the chair by an escaping rush of hot air. His body spins around the room backward, bumping on and off things as it deflates and shrinks. I can't tell if he's shouting something underneath the blast of air. I try to follow the quick crooked path of flight his shrinking body takes, but it's too fast and erratic. When all the air has escaped he falls on the ground and I can recognize his color scheme in the flattened plastic balloon.

We've been talking about Napoleon. You wonder why I'm obsessed with him and why I can't let him go. We see how he is Jerry, but I don't believe he's just Jerry. I don't think of Jerry by himself, or what he's like or was, but I know that he is part of Napoleon. You warn me against fabricating a mythology and not being able to control it. You warn me that I mustn't think I know everything, or that history repeats itself in the same way (I try to remember where I've heard that before, but I can't). You say you're worried because I seem to be less open with you. You say I seem like I'm always thinking of something else that I don't tell you. You say I sleep terribly these days and you wonder what it is. You say, "Tell me. I want to know. I care about it."

And I say, "Napoleon," and you say, "Look, don't give me that. Trust me, dammit. What is it really?" and I say, "Napoleon." And you're upset with me and you say, "Listen to me. *I'm* not Napoleon. You can trust me. Just tell me. What is it?"

And I want to say Napoleon again because that's all I know, but I know you don't want to hear it again, so I say, "I don't know," and you say, "Christ, why are you so obsessed? Why can't you just forget Napoleon? Why do you have to make up this mythology about yourself that isn't even true and torment yourself and cover up what's really there? Dammit, I wish you would kill him and get rid of him for good." And I believe that you love me and I want to say thank you and I want to kill Napoleon. I want to kill him for you.

And that night, you kill Napoleon.

There is no setting. Just white space and he's standing there with his back to me. I have a revolver and I'm aiming, but I can't pull the trigger. I realize all the messes I have made trying to kill him. Then you're there and you say, "All you have to do is pull the trigger," and you take the revolver from me and plant one clean, beautiful, silent bullet in the back of his shiny, black hair. When the smoke clears, there's no sign of anything, just clean and white and everything is clean and beautiful.

I wake up instantly and everything is quiet and beautiful.

I don't dream about Napoleon for months or think about him. Everything is good except I'm thinking of something else that I don't know and then I start joking about Napoleon, and one day you tell me you're afraid that I'm letting my imagination run away with me. You're afraid of something in the way I laugh about him, that I don't dream about him, but I think about him when I'm awake still. Like I'm making a conscious effort. You tell me you wish I could be more trusting and strong and believing. You say you're afraid of my being secretive and you wish you had more feeling of being trusted. You say you think I fear you and you wish we didn't live with that, that it's not healthy or constructive.

Then you ask me if you can borrow forty dollars because you and Terry want to get to know each other better. You tell me you two want to spend more time with each other, and this weekend you want to go away together. And I say yes, and I think of something I want to tell you when you get back, but I don't know what it is. Then I have this dream.

It's raining and I've forgotten his name. I go walking through the streets of Paris and asking everyone if they've seen a short, almost pudgy little man with a red vest, white stretch pants, black waistcoat with tails, black shiny boots, and slicked-down hair. Then I add that they might not have been able to see any of those clothes because of his large, heavy, navy coat. No one has seen him and I can't remember his name. No one understands how vital it is that I find him. They don't know that I have to kill him. It's a night like in a Victor Hugo novel, black and grey and wet, and I feel like a sewer rat and I'm looking for this little man whose name I've forgotten. I can't believe his name has slipped my mind. I remember everything about him: his coin, his clothes, the snap of his boots, how he plays cards, the money he's borrowed from me. But I can't think of his name. I keep looking because I have to kill him. I have a pistol. It's large and heavy and has a hard wooden handle. I have to be careful because I have only one bullet and I'm afraid the powder and bullet might fall out. Then I run into an alley and I see someone from behind in a large, heavy, navy coat. He's talking to someone. Very intimately leaning over and whispering. I think their bodies are touching each other. I stop dead and hear myself breathe. The person in the coat knows I'm there and knows who I am because I hear his voice and it says, "I'm not Napoleon," and then I remember his name. He doesn't move though, but stays still with the other person, only moving slightly, and I don't know what to do. He said he wasn't Napoleon, but I recognize the coat and know that only Napoleon would realize that I was looking for him and say, "I'm not Napoleon." I know that if I don't kill him now, I never will, but then I wonder, what if this person isn't Napoleon, and then he says it again: "I'm not Napoleon," still not turning toward me and I can't see his face. Then I reason that, definitely, only Napoleon would know I was looking for him, so this must be him. I feel my body tense and I pull out the gun. I set the trigger back and start to pull. Then he turns around.

The alley is dark and he moves quickly and his head is covered with a hood and I'm so upset about the gun that I can't see well, but I've already started to fire and the bullet's already going when I think I recognize him. And it's not Napoleon, and it's not Jerry; it's you.

I snap my eyes closed and scream and I don't know if the bullet hits or if it even goes off or if the blast is only the sound of my own screaming and the quick red of my hard-clenched eyes and if I've really done it.

A GOOD MAN

Jim calls me in the afternoon to ask if I can give him a ride to the doctor's tomorrow because this flu thing he has is hanging on and he's decided to get something for it. I tell him I'm supposed to be going down to Olympia to help Ange and Jean remodel their spare room and kitchen. He says it's no big deal, he can take the bus. But then a couple hours later he calls me back and says could I take him now because he really isn't feeling well. So I get in my car and go over and pick him up.

Jim stands inside the front door to the building. When he opens the door I start. His face is splotched. Sweat glistens in his week-old beard. He leans in the door frame breathing hard. He holds a brown paper grocery bag. The sides of the bag are crumpled down to make a handle. He looks so small, like a school boy being sent away from home.

"I'm not going to spend the night there," he mumbles, "but I'm bringing some socks and stuff in case."

He hobbles off the porch, his free hand grabbing the railing. I reach to take the paper bag, but he clutches it tight.

We drive to Swedish hospital and park near the Emergency Room. I lean over to hug him before we get out of the car. He's wearing four layers — T-shirt, long underwear, sweatshirt, his jacket. But when I touch his back I feel the sweat through all his clothes.

"I put these on just before you came." He sounds embarrassed.

I put an arm around him to help him inside. When he's standing at the check-in desk, I see the mark the sweat makes on his jacket.

Jim hands me the paper bag. I take his arm as we walk to the examination room to wait for a doctor. We walk slowly. Jim shuffles and I almost expect him to make his standard crack about the two of us growing old together in the ancient homos home for the prematurely senile, pinching all the candy stripers' butts, but he doesn't.

He sits down on the bed in the exam room. After he catches his breath he says, "Nice drapes."

There aren't any drapes. The room is sterile and white. Jim leans back in the chair and breathes out hard. The only other sound is the fluorescent light. He coughs.

"Say something, Tonto. Tell me story."

" — I . . . uh . . ."

I pick up a packet of tongue depressers. "Hey, look at all these. How many you think they go through in a week?"

He doesn't answer.

I take an instrument off a tray. "How 'bout this?" I turn to show him but his eyes are closed. I put it back down. When I close my mouth, the room is so quiet.

I can't tell stories the way Jim can.

A doctor comes in. She introduces herself as Dr. Allen and asks Jim the same questions he's just answered at the front desk — his fevers, his sweats, his appetite, his breath. She speaks softly, touching his arm as she listens to his answers. Then she pats his arm and says she'll be back in a minute.

In a few seconds a nurse comes in and starts poking Jim's arm to hook him up to an IV. Jim is so dehydrated she can't find the vein. She pokes him three times before one finally takes. Jim's arm is white and red. He lies there with his eyes closed, flinching.

Then Dr. Allen comes back with an other doctor who asks Jim the same questions again. The doctors ask me to wait in the private waiting room because they want to do some tests on Jim. I kiss his forehead before I leave. "I'm down the hall, Jim."

Jim waves, but doesn't say anything. They close the door.

Half an hour later, Dr. Allen comes to the waiting room. She's holding a box of Kleenex.

"Are you his sister?"

I start to answer, but she puts her hand on my arm to

stop me.

"I want you to know that hospital administration does not look favorably upon our giving detailed medical information about patients out to non-family members. And they tend to look the other way if family members want to stay past regular visiting hours."

"So," I say, "I'm his sister."

"Good. Right. OK, we need to do some more tests on Jim and give him another IV, so he needs to stay the night." She pauses. "He doesn't want to. I think he needs to talk to you."

She hands me the box of Kleenex.

Jim is lying on his back, his free elbow resting over his eyes. I walk up to him and put my hand on his leg.

"Hi."

He looks up at me, then up at the IV.

"I have to have another one of these tonight so I need to stay."

I nod.

"It's not the flu. It's pneumonia."

I nod again, and keep nodding as if he were still talking. I hear the whirr of the electric clock, the squeak of nurses' shoes in the hall.

"I haven't asked what kind."

"No."

He looks at me. I take his sweaty hand in mine.

"I don't mind going," he says, "Or being gone. But I don't want to suffer long. I don't want to take a long time going."

I try to say something to him, but I can't. I want to tell him a story, but I can't say anything.

Because I've got this picture in my head of Jim's buddy Scotty, who he grew up with in Fort Worth. And I'm seeing the three of us watching "Dynasty," celebrating the new color box Jim bought for Scotty to watch at home, and I'm seeing us getting loaded on cheap champagne, and the way Scotty laughed and coughed from under the covers and had to ask me or Jim to refill his glass or light his Benson & Hedges because he was too weak to do it himself. Then I'm seeing Jim and me having a drink the day after Scotty went, and how Jim's hands shook when he opened the first pack of cigarettes we ever shared, and how a week later Jim clammed up, just clammed right up in the middle of telling me about cleaning out Scotty's room. And I think, from the way Jim isn't talking, from the way his hand is shaking in mine, that he is seeing Scotty too.

Scotty took a long time going.

Jim stays the night at Swedish. The next night. The next.

He asks me to let some people know — his office, a few friends. Not his parents. He doesn't want to worry them. He asks me to bring him stuff from his apartment — clothes, books. I ask him if he wants his watercolors. He says no.

I go to see him every day. I bring him the *Times,* the *Blade, Newsweek.* It's easy for me to take off work. I only work as a temporary and I hate my jobs anyway, so I just don't call in. Jim likes having people visit, and lots of people come. Chubby Bob with his pink, bald head. Dale in his banker's suit. Mike the bouncer in his bomber jacket. Cindy and Bill on their way back out to Vashon. A bunch of guys from the baseball team. Denise and her man Chaz. Ange and Jeannie call him from Olympia.

We play a lot of cards. Gin rummy. Hearts when there are enough of us. Spades. Poker. We use cut-up tongue depressors for chips. I offer to bring real ones, but Jim gets a kick out of coloring them red and blue and telling us he is a very, very, very wealthy Sugar Daddy. He also gets a big kick out of cheating.

We watch a lot of tube. I sit on the big green plastic chair by the bed. Or Dale sits on the big green chair, me on his lap, and Bob on the extra folding metal chair: We watch reruns, sitcoms, *Close Encounters*. Ancient, awful Abbot and Costellos. Miniseries set between the wars. But Jim's new favorites are hospital soaps. He becomes an instant expert on everything — all the characters' affairs, the tawdry turns of plots, the long-lost illegitimate kids. He sits up on his pillows and rants about how stupid the dialogue is, how unrealistic the gore:

"Oh come on. I could do a better gun-shot wound with a paint-by-numbers set!

"Is that supposed to be a bruise?! Yo mama, pass me the hammer now. Now!

"If that's the procedure for a suture, I am Betty Grable's legs."

He narrates softly in his stage aside: "Enter tough-as-nails head nurse. Exit sensitive young intern. Enter political appointment in admin, a shady fellow not inspired by a noble urge to help his fellow human. Enter surgeon with a secret. Exit secretly addicted pharmacist."

Then during commercials he tells us gossip about the staff here at Swedish which is far juicier than anything on TV. We howl at his trashy tales until he shushes us when the show comes back on. We never ask if what he says is true. And even if we did, Jim wouldn't tell us.

But most of the time, because I'm allowed to stay after hours as his sister, it's Jim and me alone. We stare up at the big color box, and it stares down at us like the eye of God. Sometimes Jim's commentary drifts, and sometimes he is silent. Sometimes when I look over and his eyes are closed, I get up to switch off the set, but he blinks and says, "I'm not asleep. Don't turn it off. Don't go." Because he doesn't want to be alone.

Then, more and more, he sleeps and I look up alone at the plots that end in nothing, at the almost true-to-life colored shapes, at the hazy ghosts that trail behind the bodies when they move.

Jim and I met through the temporary agency. I'd lost my teaching job and he'd decided to quit bartending because he and Scotty were becoming fanatics about their baseball team and consequently living really clean. This was good for me because I was trying, well, I was thinking I really ought to try, to clean it up a bit myself. Anyway, Jim and I had lots of awful jobs together — filing, answering phones, xeroxing, taking coffee around to arrogant fat-cat lawyers, stuffing envelopes, sticking number labels on pages and pages of incredibly stupid documents, then destroying those same documents by feeding them through the shredder. The latter was the only of these jobs I liked; I liked the idea of it. I like being paid five bucks an hour to turn everything that someone else had done into pulp.

After a while, Jim got a real, permanent job, with benefits, at one of these places. But I couldn't quite stomach the thought of making that kind of commitment.

We stayed in touch though. Sometimes I'd work late xeroxing and Jim would come entertain me and play on the new color copier. He came up with some wild things — erasing bits, then painting over them, changing the color combos, double copying. All this from a machine that was my sworn enemy for eight hours a day. We'd have coffee or go out to a show or back to their place so Scotty could try out one of his experiments in international cuisine on us before he took it to the restaurant. Also, Jim helped me move out of my old apartment.

But Jim and I really started hanging out together a lot after Scotty. Jim had a bunch of friends, but I think he wanted not to be around where he and Scotty had been together so much: the dinner parties and dance bars, the clubs, the baseball team. So he chose to run around with me. To go out drinking.

We met for a drink the day after Scotty. Then a week later, we did again. Over the third round Jim started to tell me about cleaning out Scotty's room. But all the sudden he clammed up, he just clammed right up and left. He wouldn't let me walk home with him. I tried calling him but he wouldn't answer.

Then a couple weeks later he called me and said, "Wanna go for a drink?" like nothing had happened.

We met at Lucky's. I didn't say anything about what he had started to talk about the last time we'd met, and he sure didn't mention it. Well, actually, maybe he did. We always split our tab, and this round was going to be mine. But when I reached for my wallet, he stopped me.

"This one's on me, Tonto."

"Tonto?"

"The Lone Ranger." He pointed to himself. "Rides again."

He clinked his glass to mine. "So saddle up, Tonto. We're going for a ride."

We had a standing date for Friday, six o'clock, the Lucky. With the understanding that if either of us got a better offer, we just wouldn't show up and the other would know to stop waiting about 6:30 or so. However, neither of us ever got a better offer. But we had a great time talking predator. We'd park ourselves in a corner behind our drinks and eye the merchandise. Me scouting guys for him; him looking at women for me.

"He's cute. Why don't we ask him to join us."

"Not my type . . . but mmm-mmm-mmm I think somebody likes you. "

"Who?"

"That one."

"Jim, I've never see her before in my life."

"I think she likes you."

"I think she looks like a donkey. But hey, he looks really sweet. Go on, go buy him a drink."

A few times I showed up at six and saw Jim already ensconced in our corner charming some innocent, unsuspecting woman he was planning to spring on me. I usually did an abrupt about-face out of Lucky's. But one time he actually dragged me to the table to meet whoever she was. Fortunately that evening was such a disaster he didn't try that tactic again.

After a while our standing joke began to wear a little thin. I cooled it on eyeballing guys for him, but he kept teasing me, making up these incredible stories about my wild times with every woman west of the Mississippi. It bugged me for a while, but I didn't say anything. For starters, Jim wasn't the kind of guy you said shut-up to. And then, after a longer while, I realized he wasn't talking just to entertain us. His talk, his ploys to find someone for me, were his attempts to make the story of a good romance come true. Jim had come to the conclusion that neither he, nor many of his brotherhood, could any longer hope to live the good romance. He told me late one bleary, double-whiskey night, "Us boys are looking at the ugly end of the Great Experiment, Tonto. I sure hope you girls don't get in a mess like us. Ya'll will be OK, won't you? Won't ya'll girls be OK?"

Because Jim still desired, despite what he'd been through with Scott, despite how his dear brotherhood was crumbling, that some of his sibling outlaws would find good love and live in that love openly, and for a good long time, a longer time than he and Scott had had. He wanted this for everyone who marched 3rd Avenue each June, for everyone that he considered family.

He's sitting up against his pillows. I toss him the new *Texas Monthly* and kiss him hello on the forehead. He slaps his hands down on the magazine and in his sing-song voice says, "I think someone likes you!"

I roll my eyes.

He gives me his bad-cat grin. "Don't you want to know who?"

"I bet you'll tell me anyway."

"Dr. Allen."

"Oh come on, Jim, she's straight."

"And how do you know, Miss Lock-Up-Your-Daughters? Just because she doesn't wear overalls and a workshirt."

"Jim, you're worse than a Republican."

"I am, I am a wicked wicked boy. I must not disparage the Sisterhood." He flings his skinny hand up in a fist. "Right On Sister!"

I try not to laugh.

"Still, what if Dr. Allen is a breeder? I'm sure she'd be very interested in having you impart to her The Love Secrets of the Ancient Amazons."

"Jim, I'm not interested . . ."

"Honey, I been watching you. I seen you scratching. I

know you be itchin' fer some bitchin'.'"

He makes it hard not to laugh.

"Jim, if you don't zip it up, I'll have to shove a bedpan down your throat."

"In that case I'm even more glad it's about time for Dr. Allen's rounds. She'll be able to extract it from me with her maaaar-velous hands."

And in sails Dr. Allen, a couple of interns in tow.

I get up to leave.

"Oh, you don't have to leave." She smiles at me. "This is just a little check-in with Jim."

Jim winks at me behind her back.

I sit down in the folding metal chair by the window and look at downtown, at Elliott Bay, the slate gray water, the thick white sky. But I also keep looking back as Dr. Allen feels Jim's pulse, his forehead, listens to his chest. She asks him to open his mouth. She asks him how it's going today.

"Terrific. My lovely sister always cheers me up. She's such a terrific woman, you know."

I stare out the window as hard as I can.

Dr. Allen says how nice it is that Jim has such nice visitors, then tells him she'll see him later.

"See you," she says to me as she leaves.

"Yeah, see you."

The second she's out the door, Jim says, more loudly than he usually talks, "That cute Dr. Allen is such a terrific woman!"

"Jim!!" I shush him.

"And so good with her hands," he grins. "Don't you

think she's cute? I think she's cute. Almost as cute as you are when you blush."

I turn away and stare out the window again. Sure I'm blushing. And sure, I'm thinking about Dr. Allen. But what I'm thinking is why, when she was looking at him, she didn't say, "You're looking good today, Jim." Or, "You're coming right along, Jim." Or "We're gonna have to let you out of here soon, Jim, you're getting too healthy for us."

Why won't she tell him something like that?

There's a wheelchair in his room. Shiny stainless steel frame, padded leather seat. Its arms look like an electric chair.

He's so excited he won't let me kiss him hello.

"That's Silver. Your dear friend Dr. Allen says I can go out for some fresh air today."

"Really?" I'm skeptical. He's hooked to an IV again.

"Gotta take advantage of the sun. Saddle up, Tonto."

He presses the buzzer. In a couple of minutes an aide comes in to transfer the IV from his bed to the pole sticking up from the back of the chair. The drip bag hangs like a toy. I help Jim into his jacket and cap, put a cover across his lap and slide his hospital slippers up over his woolly socks.

"Are you sure you feel up to this?"

"Sure I'm sure. And if I don't get a cup of non-hospital coffee, I am going to lynch someone."

"OK, OK, I'll be back in a minute. I gotta go to the bathroom."

I go to the nurses' station.

"Can Jim really go out today?"

The guy at the desk looks up.

"Dr. A says it's fine. You guys can go across the street to Rex's or something. A lot of patients do. They uh . . . don't have the same rules as the hospital." He puckers his lips and puts two fingers up to mime smoking.

"Uh-huh. Got it."

Back in the room I take the black plastic handles of the chair and start to push.

Jim flings his hand in the air, "Hi-Yo Silver!"

I wheel him into the hall, past doctors and aides in clean white coats, past metal trays full of plastic buckets and rubber gloves and neat white stacks of linens. Past skinny guys shuffling along in housecoats and slippers.

The elevator is huge, wide enough to carry a couple of stretchers. Jim and I are the only ones in it. I feel like we're the only people in a submarine, sinking down to some dense, cold otherworld where we won't be able to breathe. Jim watches the elevator numbers. I watch the orange reflection of the lights against his eyes.

When the elevator opens to the bustling main entrance foyer, his eyes widen. It isn't as white and quiet as he's gotten used to. In his attempt to tell himself he isn't so bad off, he's made himself forget what health looks like. I see him stare, wide-eyed and silent, as a man runs across the foyer to hug a friend, as a woman bends down to pick up a kid. I push him slowly across the foyer in case he wants to change his mind.

When the electric entry doors slide open he gasps.

"Let's blow this popcorn stand, baby." He nods across the street to Rex's. "Carry me back to the ol' saloon."

I push him out to the sidewalk. It's rougher than the slick floor of the building. Jim grips the arms of the wheelchair. We wait at the crosswalk for the light to change, Jim hunching in his wheelchair in the middle of a crowd of people standing. People glance at him then glance away. I look down at the top of his cap, the back of his neck, his shoulders.

When the light changes everyone surges across Madison. I ease the chair down where the sidewalk dips then push him into the pedestrian crossing. We're the only ones left in the street when the light turns green.

"Get a move on, Silver."

The wheels tremble, the metal rattles, the IV on the pole above him shakes. The liquid shifts. Jim's hands tighten like an armchair football fan's. His veins stand up. He sticks his head forward as if he could help us move. I push us to the other side.

We clatter into Rex's. There's the cafeteria line and a bunch of chairs and tables. I steer him to an empty table, pull a chair away and slide him in.

"Jesus," he mumbles, "I feel like a kid in a high chair."

"Coffee?"

"Yeah. And a packet of Benson & Hedges."

"Jim."

"Don't argue. If God hadn't wanted us to smoke, he wouldn't have created the tobacco lobby."

"Jim."

"For god's sake Tonto, what the hell difference will a cigarette make?"

While I stand in line, I glance at him. He's looking out the long wall of windows to Madison, watching people walk by on their own two feet, all the things they carry in their hands — briefcases, backpacks, shopping bags, umbrellas. The people in Rex's look away from him. I'm glad we're only across the street from the hospital.

I put the tray on the table in front of him. He puts his hand out for his coffee, but can't quite reach it. I hand him his cup and take mine.

"Did you get matches?"

"Light up."

"It's good to be out . . . So tell me, Tonto, how's the wild west been in my absence?"

"Oh, you know, same as ever . . ."

"Don't take it lightly, pardner. Same as ever is a fucking miracle."

I don't know whether to apologize or not.

When we finish our cigarettes, he points. "Another."

I light him one.

"You shouldn't smoke so much," he says as I light another for myself.

"What?! You're the one who made me haul you across the street for a butt."

"And you drink too much."

"Jim, get off my case."

He pauses. "You've got something to lose, Tonto."

I look away from him.

He sighs. "We didn't use to be so bad, did we Tonto? When did we get so bad?"

I don't say, After Scotty.

He shakes his head as if he could shake away what he is thinking. "So clean it up, girl. As a favor to the Ranger? As a favor to the ladies? Take care of that luscious body-thang of yours. Yes? Yes?"

I roll my eyes.

"Promise?"

"Jim . . ." I never make promises; nobody ever keeps them.

"Promise me."

I shrug a shrug he could read as a no or yes. He knows it's all he'll get from me. He exhales through his nose like a very disappointed maiden aunt. Then slowly, regretfully, pushes the cigarettes towards me.

"These are not for you to smoke. They're for you to keep for me because La Dottoressa and her dancing Kildairettes won't let anyone keep them in the hospital. So I am entrusting them to you to bring for me when we have our little outings. And I've counted them; I'll know if you steal any."

"OK."

"Girl Scouts' honor?"

"OK, OK."

The cellophane crackles when I slip them into my jacket.

"Now. Back to the homestead, Tonto."

The Riding Days:

One hung-over morning when Jim and I were swaying queasily on the very crowded number 10 bus to downtown, I bumped into, literally, Amy. She was wearing some incredible perfume.

"Hi," I tried to sound normal. I gripped the leather ceiling strap tighter. "What are you doing out at this hour? On the bus?"

"Well, the Nordie's sale is starting today and I want to be there early. But Brian's car is in the shop so he couldn't drop me off."

"Jeez. Too bad."

"Oh, it's not that bad. He'll be getting a company car today to tide us over."

"How nice."

She smiled her pretty smile at Jim but I didn't introduce them. She got off at the Nordstrom stop.

After she got off, Jim said, "She's cute, why don't you — "

"She's straight," I snapped. "She's a breeder. Now. She used to be the woman I used to live with. In the old apartment."

"The one you've never told me about," he said.

I stared into the back of the coat of the man squished in front of me. "Jim, shut up."

"I'm sorry, babe . . ." He tried to put his arm around me. I wriggled away from him.

"Hey, she's not that cute," he said when I jumped off the bus at the next stop. It was several blocks from work, but I wanted to walk.

That afternoon, Jim sent me a box of chocolates. The

chocolates were delivered to me in the xerox room. They were delivered with a card. "Forget the ugly bitch. Eat us instead, you luscious thang." I shared the chocolates with the office. They made the talk, the envy of the office for a week. I kept the contents of the card a secret.

Jim sweet-talked my apartment manager into letting him into my tiny little studio apartment so he could leave me six — *six* — vases of flowers around my room when I turned twenty-seven. He taught me how to iron shirts. He wore a top hat when we went to see the Fred and Ginger festival at the U. He knew that the solution for everything, for almost everything, was a peanut butter and guacamole sandwich. He placed an ad in the *Gay News* for Valentine's Day which said, "Neurotic lesbian still on rebound seeks females for short, intense, physical encounters. No breeders." And my phone number. Then let me stay at his place and laughed at me because I was afraid the phone might ring. He brought me horrible instant cinnamon and fake apple fla-vored oatmeal the mornings I slept on his couch, the mornings after we'd both had more than either of us could handle and didn't want to be in our apartments alone, and said, "This'll zap your brain into gear, Mrs. Frankenstein," and threw me a clean, fresh, ironed shirt to wear to work. He fed Trudy his whole-food hippie cookies to keep her quiet so he and I could sneak out to Jean and Ange's porch for a cigarette and a couple of draws on the flask.

He wore his ridiculous bright green bermuda shorts and wagged his ass like crazy, embarrassing the hell out of me, at the Gay Pride March. He raised his fist and yelled, "Ride

On, Sister, Ride On!" to the Dykes on Bikes. He slapped high-heeled, mini-skirted queens on the back and said in a husky he-man voice, "Keep the faith, brother." I got afraid some guy might slap him or hit him with his purse, or some woman might slug him. When I started to say something, Jim stopped. The march kept streaming down 3rd Avenue beside us. The June sun hit me on the head and Jim glared at me. He crossed his arms across his chest like he was trying to keep from yelling.

"Tonto, what the hell are you afraid of anyway? You may like to think of us all as a bunch of unbalanced, volatile perverts, but every single screaming fairy prancing down this boulevard and every last one of you pissed-off old Amazons is my family. My kith and my kin and my kind. My siblings. Your siblings. And if you're so worried about their behavior you should just turn your chickenshit ass around and crawl back into the nearest closet because you are on the wrong fucking ride."

I didn't say anything. He stared at me several seconds. Then a couple of punky women dancing to their boom box dragged Jim along with them. I watched their asses wag off in front of me. I started to walk. But I was ashamed to march with him again. Then, when he saw the Educational Service District workers contingent in front of us, their heads covered in paper sacks because you can still be fired from your state school teaching job for being queer, Jim turned around and hollered, "At least you don't have to keep your sweet gorgeous sexy face covered like that anymore, Tonto." I stared at my pathetic, scared, courageous former colleagues. Jim pranced back to me and yanked me into a chorus line where everyone, all these brave, tough pansies, these heroic, tender dykes, had their arms around each others' backs. Jim pulled me along. I felt the firmness of his chest against my shoulder.

"This is the way it's gonna be, Tonto. Someday it's all gonna be this great."

He laughed at his own stories and he clapped at his own jokes. And he never, never, despite how many times I asked, told me which stories he'd made up, which ones were true.

And sometimes, when he's holding court from his hospital bed, and he's in the middle of telling us some outrageous story, making all of us laugh, and we're all laughing, I forget. When he's telling it like there's no tomorrow — no — like there *is* — I just forget how he is in his body.

He gets over something, then gets something else. Then he gets better then he gets worse. Then he begins to look OK and says he's ready to go home. Then he gets worse. Then he gets something else.

On the days they think he's up to it, they let me take him out. A couple times both of us walk, but other times he rides. They call it his constitutional. We call it his faggot break.

I bring him a cup of Rex's coffee and throw the cigarettes across the table to him. He counts them, purses his lips and says, "You *are* a good Girl Scout." Then he leans toward me, gestures like a little old lady for me to put my ear up close to him.

"She's just trying to make you jealous." he whispers.

"What?"

"Doc-tor A-llen," he mouths silently.

He nods across Rex's to a table in the no-smoking section. Dr. Allen is having a cup of coffee with a woman.

"She knows we come here, she hopes you'll see her with another woman and be forced to take action."

"Jim . . ."

I'm sure Dr. Allen has seen us, Jim and me and the cigarettes, but I'm hoping she's taking a break from being doctor long enough to not feel obliged to come over and give Jim some healthy advice.

"She likes you *very much*, you know."

"Jim, I've probably had five minutes of conversation with the woman," I whisper, "all about you."

"Doesn't matter. It's chemistry. Animal maaag-netism."

He wants me to laugh.

"Come on, Jim. Give it a rest . . ."

He turns around to look at Dr. Allen. Then he looks back at me. He takes a long drag on his cigarette. He tries to sound buoyant. "Hey, I'm just trying to get you a buddy, Tonto. Who you gonna ride with when the Ranger's gone?"

One time Jim told me, this is what he said, he said, "A lie is what you tell when you're a chicken shit. But a story is what you tell for good."

"Even if it isn't true?"

"It's true. If you tell a story for good, it's true."

I had had them twice and they were always great. They truly, truly may have been the best sour cream enchiladas on the planet. But that time, after two bites, Jim threw down his fork.

"These suck."

"Jim, they're fine."

"They suck."

He pushed the plate away. "I can't eat this shit."

I handed him the hot sauce and the guacamole. "Add a little of these."

"I said I cannot eat this crap." He lifted his hands like he was trying to push something away. I started to clear the table.

"Leave it. *Leave it.*"

I put the plate down. I looked away from him. Then at him. "Let's go out for Chinese."

He didn't say anything, just nodded.

I ordered everything: egg rolls, hot and sour soup, moo goo gai pan, garlic pork, veg, rice, a few beers. He asked me to tell him a story and I did. A lewd, insulting, degrading tale about a guy at the temp agency, a swishy little closet case we both despised. I told about him being caught, bare-assed, his pecker in his paw, in the 35th floor supply room by one of the directors. Jim adored the story. He laughed really loud. He laughed until he cried. He didn't ask if it was true.

We ate everything. All the plum sauce. All the little crackers. Every speck of rice. But we didn't open our fortune cookies.

On the way home, Jim put his arm around me and said, "You're learning, Tonto."

The enchiladas were a recipe of Scotty's.

The door is half closed. I take one step in. There's a sweeping sound in the room, a smell. The curtain has been drawn around the bed. I see a silhouette moving.

"Jim?"

"Go away." His voice is little. "I made a mess."

An aide in a white coat peeks around the curtain. He's holding a mop. He's wearing plastic gloves, a white mask over his mouth and nose. I leave.

I go up to the Rose. Rosie sees me coming through the door. She's poured a schooner for me by the time I reach the bar.

"Jesus, woman." She leans over the bar to look at me as I'm climbing onto the barstool.

"Shrunken body, shrunken head . . . gonna be nothing left of you soon, girl."

I reach for the beer. She stops my hand.

"We don't serve alcohol alone. You have to order something to eat with it."

"Gimme a break, Rosie. I have one dollar and — " I fish into my jeans, "55 . . . 56 . . . 57 cents."

"Sorry pal. It's policy."

"Since when."

"Since now. It's a special policy for you."

"Rosie, please."

"Don't mess with the bartender."

I drop my face into my hands. "Please Rosie."

She lifts my chin and looks at me. "If you promise to clean your plate, we'll put it on your tab."

"You don't run tabs."

She points to her chest. "I'm the boss."

As I'm finishing my beer she slaps a plate in front of me — a huge bacon-cheeseburger with all the trimmings. A mound of fries. A pint glass of milk.

She writes out the bill and pockets it. "We'll talk."

"Thanks."

I take a bite. She puts her elbows on the bar.

"How's Jim."

"The same." My mouth is full.

She cocks her head.

I swallow. "Worse."

"Jeez . . ." She touches my arm. "Eat, honey. Eat something."

I eat. Sesame seed bun. Bacon. Mustard. Lettuce. Pickles. Tomatoes. Cheese. Meat. Grease on my fingers. I chew and swallow. It is so easy.

Jim on the drip-feed. Jim not keeping anything down. Or shitting it out in no time. His throat and asshole sore from everything that comes up, that runs through him. His oozy mouth. His bloody gums.

A hand on my back. "Hi."

I turn and almost choke.

"You're Jim's — "

I nod. "Yeah, right." I swallow. "You're Doctor Allen. Hi."

I wipe my mouth and hands on the napkin.

She's saying to the woman she's with, "This is Jim's sister," as if her friend's already heard of Jim. Or of me. Dr. Allen extends her hand to me. "Please, my name's Patricia."

I shake her hand.

"And this is my sister Amanda. It's her first time here — I mean — here in Seattle." She does this nervous little laugh. "She's visiting from Buffalo."

It's the woman she was having coffee with at Rex's.

"Oh Buffalo," I say, "How nice."

"I've come to see if poor Pat's life is really as boring as she tells me it is. Doesn't have to be does it?" the sister says with a grin.

I don't know what to answer. I do this little laugh.

They both look around the bar. Not wide, serious check-out sweeps of their heads, but shy quick glances. They certainly aren't old hands at this. And I think I see two different varieties of nerves here. I try to read which is the tolerant, supportive sister, and which is the one who wanted to come to this particular bar in the first place.

"Mind if we join you?"

"Uh, no. Sure. Great."

I gesture to the empty barstool next to me, then I stand up and gesture to my own. "But I was just going, actually . . . here, have my stool." I down half the glass of milk. "Gotta be at work early in the morning," I lie.

They look at each other and at me. I feel like one of them's about to laugh, but I don't know which. Dr. Allen sits on my stool. Jim's right. She is pretty cute.

I gulp down the rest of the milk, slap my hands on the bar and shout into the kitchen, "I owe you Rosie!"

I say to the sister, "Nice to meet you. Have a nice time in Seattle." And to the Doctor, "Nice to bump into you. See you 'round."

Then I'm standing outside on the sidewalk, shaking.

Because maybe, if I had stayed there in the bar with them, and had them buy me a beer or two, or coaxed a couple more out of Rosie, maybe I would have asked, "So which of you is the supportive sister, and which of you is the dyke?" Or maybe I would have asked, "So how 'bout it ladies. Into which of your lovely beds might I more easily insinuate myself?"

Or maybe I would have asked — no — no — but maybe I would have asked, "So, Dr. Allen, you are pretty cute, how 'bout it. How long 'til Jim goes?"

I bring him magazines and newspapers. The *Times,* the *Blade,* the *Body Politic.* They all run articles. Apparent answers, possible solutions, almost cures. Experiments and wonder drugs. A new technique. But more and more the stories are of failures. False starts. The end of hope.

Bob's been coughing the last few times he's been here. He's still at it today.

Bob coughs. I look at Dale. He looks away.

One evening in the middle of "Marcus Welby," Jim announces, "I'm bored outta my tits, girls. I wanna have a party."

Mike, who's been drooping in front of the TV set, sits up.

"I say I am ready for a paaaaar-tay!"

Mike says, "Jimmy boy, you're on."

We OK it with Dr. Allen. Mike raids the stationery store on Broadway for paper hats and confetti and party favors and cards. We call everyone and it's on for the evening after next. They limit the number of people allowed in a room at a time so Mike and and I take turns hanging out by the elevator to do crowd control. Jim shrieks, he calls me "Tonto the Bouncer" and flexes his arm in a skinny little she-man biceps. It's great to see everybody, and everyone brings Jim these silly presents: an inflatable plastic duck, a shake-up scene of the Space Needle, a couple of incredibly ugly fuzzy animals, a bouquet of balloons. Somebody brings him a child's watercolor set; it's the only gift he doesn't gush about.

When I start to clean the wrapping paper, he says, "Oh leave it a while." He likes the shiny colors and the rustling sound the paper makes when he shifts in bed.

When anybody leaves, he blows a kiss and says, "Bye-bye cowpoke," "Happy Trails."

He knows what he's doing.

I see it when I'm coming down the hall, a laminated sign on the door of his room. I tiptoe the last few yards because I don't want him to hear me stop to read it, acting as if I believe what it says. It's a warning, like something you'd see on a pack of cigarettes or a bottle of pesticide. It warns about the contents. It tells you not to touch.

I push myself into his room before I can give myself a chance to reconsider. I push myself towards his bed, towards his forehead to give him his regular kiss hello.

"Don't touch me."

When he pushes me away, I'm relieved.

"Do you realize they're wearing plastic gloves around me all the time now? Face masks? They've put my wallet and clothes into plastic bags. As if me and my stuff is gonna jump on 'em and bleed all over 'em, as if my sweat — "

"Jim, that's bullshit. This isn't the Middle Ages, it's 1984. And they're medical people, they should know they don't need to do that. Haven't they read — "

"Why don't you go tell 'em, Tonto? Why don't you just march right over to 'em with all your little newspaper articles and you just tell 'em the truth."

"I will, Jim, I'll — "

"Oh for fuck's sake, Tonto, they *are* medical people. They know what they're doing." He covers his eyes with a hand and says wearily, "And I know what my body is doing."

He holds his skinny white hand over his eyes. I can see the bones of his forearm, the bruises on his pale, filmy skin. He looks like an old man. The sheet rises and falls unevenly with his breath.

I ought to hold him but I don't want to.

"Jim?" I say, "Jim?" I don't know if he's listening.

Inside the belt-line of my jeans, down the middle of my

back and on my stomach, I feel myself begin to sweat. I start to babble. A rambling, unconnected pseudo-summary of articles I haven't brought him, a doctor-ed précis of inoperative statements, edited news-speak, jargon, evasions, unmeant promises, lies.

But I'm only half thinking of what I say, and I'm not thinking of Jim at all.

I'm thinking of me. And of how my stomach clutched when he said that about the sweat. I'm thinking that I want to get out of his room immediately and wash my hands and face and take a shower and boil my clothes and get so far away from him that I won't have to breathe the air he's breathed. Then further, to where he can't see how I, like everyone I like to think I'm so different from, can desert him at the drop of a hat, before the drop of a hat, because my good-girl Right-On-Sister sympathies extend only as far as my assurance of my immunity from what is killing him. But once the thought occurs to me that I might be in danger I'll be the first bitch on the block to saddle up and leave him in the dust.

I don't know what I say to him; I know I don't touch him.

After a while he offers me a seat to watch TV, but I don't sit. I tell him I've got to go. I tell him I have a date. He knows I'm lying.

I look around for Dr. Allen. She tells me she thinks this recent hospital policy is ludicrous. "It just increases everybody's hysteria. There's no evidence of contagion through casual contact. If these people . . ." But I don't listen to the rest of what she says. My mind is still repeating *no evidence of contagion through casual contact.* I'm so relieved I'm taken out of danger. I realize I'm happier than if she'd told me Jim was going to live.

I don't listen until I hear her asking me something. I don't hear the words, just the tone in her voice.

"Huh?"

She looks at me hard. Then shakes her head and turns away. She knows what I was thinking, where the line of my loyalty runs out.

The next day before I visit him, I ask Dr. Allen, "Are you sure, if I only touch him . . ."

It's the only time she doesn't look cute. She practically spits. "You won't risk anything by hugging your brother."

Her eyes make a hole in my back as I walk to his room.

I hug him very carefully, how I believe I can stay safe. He holds me longer than he usually does. He doesn't say anything, when I pull away, about the fact that I don't kiss his forehead, which shines with sweat.

"Come here," he says in his lecher voice, "Daddy's got some candy for you."

He hands me a hundred dollar bill.

"What's this?"

"What I still owe you for the TV."

"What?"

"The hundred bucks I borrowed for the color TV."

Jim wanted to buy it for Scotty when all Scotty could do was watch TV. Jim wasn't going to get paid until the end of the month so I lent it to him. He wanted to pay me back immediately but he kept having all these bills.

"Dale withdrew it from the bank for me."

"I don't want it."

He glares at me. "The Ranger is a man of honor, Tonto."

"OK, OK, but I don't want it now."

He keeps glaring. "So you want it later? You gonna ride into Wells Fargo bank and tell them part of my estate is yours?"

"Dale can — " I close my eyes.

"I owe you, Tonto. Take Dr. Allen out for the time of her life."

"Jim . . ."

"Goddammit, it's all I can do."

He grabs me by the belt loop of my jeans and tries to pull me toward him but he's too weak. I step toward the bed. He stuffs the bill into my pocket.

"Now go away please. I'm tired."

Was this a conversation? Was it a story?

I wish Scotty knew how I felt about him.

He knew.

I never told him. I wish I'd said the words.

He knew.

How do you know?

He told me.

Did he? What did he say?

Scotty told me, he said, Jim loves me.

Did he really?

Yes.

Did he say anything else?

Yes. He said, I love Jim.

He said he loved me?

More than anything.

Is that true?

Yes, Jim, it's true.

This is how I learn to tell a story.

We stay away for longer than we ought. I tell him it's time to go back, but he whines like a boy who doesn't want recess to end. He chatters. For the first time since I've known him, he starts retelling stories he has told to me before, stories that lose a lot in the retelling. But finally he runs out of things to say and lets me wheel him out of Rex's.

There's a traffic jam. Cars are backed up to Broadway and everybody's honking. A couple blocks away a moving van is trying to turn onto a narrow street. People at the crosswalk are getting impatient. They look around for cops and when they don't see any, start crossing Madison between the cars.

"I'm cold," says Jim.

He puts his free hand under his blanket. I lean down to tuck the cover more closely around his legs. His face is white.

"I'm cold," he grumbles again, "I wanna go back in."

"In a minute, Jim. We can't go yet."

"But I'm freezing." He looks up. "Where's the fucking sun anyway?"

I take my jacket off and wrap it around his shoulders. The cellophane of the cigarette package crinkles. I take care not to hit the drip feed tube.

People start laying on their horns. The poor stupid van ahead is moving forward then back, inch by inch, trying to squeeze around the corner.

"It's moving, Jim. The truck's going."

"About time," he says loudly, "Doesn't the driver realize what he's holding up here?"

Then the truck stalls. There's the gag of the engine, silence, the rev of the motor, the sputter when the engine floods.

"Someone go tell that goddamn driver what he's holding up here."

People in their cars look out at Jim.

"I've got to get back in," he screams, "Go! Go!" He starts shooing the cars with his hands. The drip feed swings.

I grab his arm. "Jim, the IV."

"Fuck the IV!" he yells, "Fuck the traffic. I'm going back in. I have to get back in."

"We're going, Jim, the traffic's moving now," I lie. "We're going in. Settle down, OK?"

He pushes himself up a couple of inches to see the truck.

"The truck isn't moving, Tonto."

He kicks his blanket awry and tries to find the ground with his feet. "I'm walking."

"Jim, you can't."

"So what am I supposed to do. Fly?"

"You're supposed to wait. When the traffic clears — "

"I'm sick of waiting. You said it was clearing. You lied to me. I'm sick of everyone lying. I'm sick of waiting. I'm sick — " His voice cracks.

I put my hand on his arm. "When the traffic clears I'm going to push you and Silver across the street."

"It's not a horse," he screams, "it's a goddamn wheel-chair!"

He starts to tremble. He grips the arms of the chair. "It's a wheelchair full of goddamn croaking faggot!" He slaps his hands over his face and whispers, "Tonto, I don't wanna. Don't let me — I don't wanna — I don't wanna — "

I put my arms around him and pull him to me. His head is against my collarbone. His cap falls off his sweaty head. I try to hold him. He lets me a couple of seconds then he tries to pull away. He isn't strong enough. But I know what he means so I pull back. He grabs my shirt, one of his.

"I don't wanna — " he cries, "I don't wanna — "

I put my hands on his back of his head and pull him to my chest.

"I don't wanna — I don't wanna — " he sobs.

His hands and face are wet. I hold his head.

He grabs me like a child wanting something good.

When we get back to his room he's still crying. I ring for Dr. Allen. Jim asks me to leave.

I pace around in the hall. When Dr. Allen comes out of his room, she says, "He's resting. He isn't good but he's not as bad as you think. He won't want to see you for a while. Now that you've seen him like this, it's harder for him to pretend he's not afraid. You can call the nurses' station tonight if you're concerned, but don't come see him till tomorrow. And call first."

I want to tell her to tell him a story, to make him not afraid.

But I don't. I say, "I'm going to call his parents."

She looks at me.

"*Our* parents," I mumble.

"He hasn't wanted his family to know?"

"Right."

"Call them."

I call his parents that night. They say they'll fly out in the morning and be able to be with him by noon. I tell them I'll book them a hotel a five minute walk from the hospital. They want to take the airport bus in themselves.

I call him in the morning.

"Hey, buddy."

"Yo Tonto."

"Listen, you want anything special today? I'm doing my Christmas shopping on the way down to see you."

"No you're not."

"Who says?"

"Santa says. I called Jean and Ange this morning and you're going down there for the week. That remodeling you were supposed to help them with way back is getting moldy. So it's the bright lights of Olympia for you, Sex-cat."

"Jim . . ."

"You have to go. They're going to pay you."

"What?!"

"They said they'd have to pay somebody, and they're afraid to have a common laborer around the priceless silver. So they want you. And it's not like you've been earning it hand over fist since you've been playing candy-striper with me."

"Jim, they don't have any money."

"They do now. Jeannie managed to lawyer-talk her way into some loot for her latest auto disaster and Ange is determined to spend the cash before Jeannie throws it away on another seedy lemon. So, Tonto, you got to go. It's your sororal duty."

It was impossible to talk Jim out of anything.

"Give my best to the girls and tell Trudy the Sentinal Bitch I said a bark is a bark is a bark."

"Doesn't Alice get a hello?"

"Alice is stupid. I will not waste my sparkling wit on her."

"OK . . ."

Were we going to get through this entire conversation without a mention of yesterday?

"So Tonto, the Ranger is much improved today. . . . My folks called a while ago from DFW airport. They're on their way to see me. Thanks for calling them."

"Sure."

"We'll see you next week then."

"Right."

He hangs up the phone before I can tell him goodbye.

I drive to Olympia. Ange is outside chopping wood. When I pull into the yard she slings the axe into the center of the block. She gives me a huge hug, her great soft arms around my back, her breasts and belly big and solid against me. She holds me a long time, kisses my hair.

"Hi baby."

"Ange."

She puts her arm around my back and brings me inside. The house smells sweet. They're baking. Jeannie blows me a kiss from the kitchen.

"Hello gorgeous!"

"Jeannie my darling."

I warm my hands by the wood stove. Ange yells at Gertrude, their big ugly German shepherd, to shut up. She's a very talkative dog. Jeannie brings in a plate of whole wheat cookies. I pick up Alice the cat from the couch and drop her on the floor. She is a stupid cat. She never protests anything. I sit on the place she's made warm on the couch. Jean hands me the plate. The cookies are still warm. I hesitate. It always amazes me they can, along with Jeannie's law school scholarship, support themselves by selling this horrible homemade hippie food to health food joints.

I take a cookie. "Thanks."

"How's Jim?"

"OK . . ."

"Bad?"

"Yeah."

"He sounded incredibly buoyant on the phone, so we figured . . . we told him we'd come up to see him next week when we've finished some of this." She nods at the cans and boards and drywall stacked up outside the spare room.

"Let's get to work."

"Yeah. Let's do it."

Ange puts an old Janis Joplin on the stereo. We knock the hell out of the walls.

They cook a very healthy dinner. As she's about to sit down, Jeannie says, "Hey, we got some beer in case you wanted one. Want one?" Ange and Jean haven't kept booze in their house for years.

"No thanks." There's a jar of some hippie fruit juice on the table. "This is fine."

They look at each other. We eat.

I sleep on the couch in the living room. Gertrude sleeps in front of the wood stove. I listen to her snort. She turns around in circles before she settles down to sleep, her head out on her paws.

Jim and I used to flip for who got the couch and who got the tatami mat on the floor next to the dog. I lean up on my elbow to look at Trudy the Sentinal Bitch. Only Jim could have re-named her that. In the bedroom Ange and Jean talk quietly.

All the junk has been moved from the spare room into the living room. Some of it is stacked at the end of the couch. I toss the blanket off me and sift through the pile. Rolled-up posters, curling photographs. There's a framed watercolor of Jim's, a scene of Ange and Jeannie by the pond, with Gertrude, fishing. They look so calm together. They didn't know Jim was painting them. They didn't know how he saw them.

I find one of all of us, three summers ago when we climbed Mount Si. Jim is tall and bearded, his arms around the three of us, me and Jeannie squished together under his left, Ange hugged under his right. All of us are smiling at the cameraman, Scotty.

Two nights later the phone rings late. I'm awake, light on, blanket off, before they've answered it. When Ange comes out of the bedroom I'm already dressed.

"That was Dr. Allen. His parents are with him. You should go."

They won't let me drive. We all pile into the truck; Jeannie driving, Ange in the middle, me against the door. Jeannie doesn't stop at the signs or the red lights. She keeps an even 80 on the highway. For once, Ange doesn't razz her about her driving.

I-5 is quiet. The only things on the road are some long-haul trucks, a few cars. We see the weak beige lights of the insides of these other cars, the foggy orange lights across the valley. We drive along past sleepy Tacoma, Federal Way, the airport.

"Look, would you guys mind if I had a cigarette?"

"Go ahead baby."

Ange reaches over me and rolls down the window. I root around in my jacket for Jim's cigarettes. I'm glad I didn't make that promise to him.

We pull into the hospital parking lot. My hand is on the door before we stop.

"You go up. We'll get Bob and Dale and meet you on the floor in ten minutes."

In the elevator is a couple a little older than me. Red-eyed and sniffling like kids. We look at each other a second then look at the orange lights going up.

When the elevator opens I run. But when I see the guys in white taking things from the room in plastic bags, I stop. The man at the nurses' station looks up.

"Your parents are in the waiting room."

"My what?"

"Your parents."

Then I remember how that first night, a million years ago, when Dr. Allen had told me she couldn't tell me about Jim unless I was in his family, I had told the story of being his sister.

"Oh Christ."

"They told me to send you in when you came."

"Oh Jesus."

They've left the waiting room door open a crack. I look in. His father is wearing an overcoat. His hands lay loose around the rim of the hat in his lap. His mother is touching her husband's arm. Neither of them is talking.

I knock on the door very lightly.

They look up.

"You must be Jim's friend. Come in."

I push the door open. They both stand up and put out their hands. I shake their hands.

"Mary Carlson."

"Jim Carlson."

I introduce myself.

"The young man at the desk told us that, before she went into surgery, Dr. Allen called our daughter and that she was on her way. But we don't have a daughter."

"I'm sorry, But I — the first night Jim was here I told Dr. Allen — "

Mr. Carlson is still shaking my hand. He squeezes it hard.

"You have nothing to apologize for. Jim told us what a good friend you'd been to him. Both after Scotty, and more recently.

"Jim was a good friend too. I'm sorry I didn't call you sooner."

"We know he asked you not to. We had a few good days with him. I think he wanted to get better before he saw us," says Mrs. Carlson. "He didn't want us to have to see him and have to wait the way he had to wait with Scotty."

"Yes."

"Did you know Scotty?"

"Yes."

"He was a lovely young man."

"He was good to Jim," says Mr. Carlson. "There were things about Jim it took us a long time to understand, but he was a good son." He says this slowly. "He was a good man."

"Yes."

"We loved him." Mr. Carlson's mouth is open like he's going to say more, but then there's this sound in his throat and he drops his face into his hands. "Dear God," he says, "Oh dear God."

Mrs. Carlson pulls her husband's head to her breast. His hat falls to the floor.

I pick the hat up off the floor and put it on the table. I leave the room. When I close the door, I hear his father crying.

Ange and Jean and Bob and Dale are standing at the nurses' station. The boys are in pj's and overcoats and house-slippers. They look at me. I look at them. We all look at each other. Nobody says anything.

Dale walks over to the wall and puts his forehead against the wall. His shoulders shake. Bob goes over and puts his hand on Dale's back. Nobody says anything.

We get in the truck to go back to Bob and Dale's. We all insist Bob sits up front with Jean and Ange. Dale and I sit in the open back. We haul the dog-smelling woolly blanket over our knees and huddle up next to each other. I can feel the cool ribbed metal of the bottom of the truck through my jeans. Jeannie pulls us away from the bright lights of the hospital onto Madison.

It's dark but there're enough breaks in the clouds that we can see a star or two. The lights are off at Rex's, the streets are empty. Jean drives so slow and cautiously, full stops at the signs and lights, and pauses at the intersections. There's not another car on the road, but I think she hopes if she does everything very carefully, things might not break apart.

Jean stops at the light on Broadway. Dale and I look into the back window of the pickup and see their three heads—

Jeannie's punky hairdo sticking up, Ange's halo of wild fuzz, Bob's shiny smooth round scalp. The collar of Bob's pj's is crooked above his housecoat. He's usually so neatly groomed, but now he looks like a rumpled, sleepy child.

Dale begins to tremble. I put my hand on his knee.

"Jim was a great guy, the greatest, but now it's like he was never here. What did he ever do that's gonna last? It's like his life was nothing."

"Jim was a good man," I say.

Dale nods.

"And he loved a good man. He loved Scotty well."

"And that's enough?"

"It's good," I say, "It's true."

Dale takes my hand. He holds it hard. It's the first time I notice he wears a ring.

He takes a breath. "Bob . . . you know Bob . . . I'm afraid maybe . . . I think Bob . . ."

He can't say it. I see his eyelashes trembling, the muscles in his jaw as he tries to keep from crying. He swallows and closes his eyes.

"Bob is a good man," says Dale.

"Yeah Dale, I know. Bob is a good man, too."

So we all go back to Bob and Dale's. I call the Carlson's hotel to leave Bob and Dale's phone number. We drink tea and sit around in the living room until someone says we ought to get some sleep.

"Well, there's plenty of pj's," says Bob. "We can have a pajama paaaaaaar-tay."

He says it before he realizes it's a Jim word. Ange and Jeannie and I try to laugh. Dale closes his eyes.

Bob and Dale get pj's for us. They wash the teacups as Ange and Jean and I change. We all look really silly in the guys' flannel pj's. When the boys come out of the kitchen and see us, they laugh. It's a real laugh. It sounds good.

Ange and Jean are going to stay in the guest room. Ange says to me, "You wanna stay with us, babe?"

Dale says, "Or you can sleep on the couch in our room."

"Thanks guys." I plop down on the living room couch. "This is fine with me."

Dale goes to the linen closet to get some sheets and blankets.

If I lie next to someone I will break apart.

I wake up first. I put the water on to boil. When Jean and Ange come out of the guest room, I say "The Katzenjammer twins."

They look at my pj's. "Triplets," Jeannie says.

"Quads," says Ange when Dale comes into the kitchen.

He gives us each a scratchy, unshaven kiss on the cheek.

"Good morning lovelies."

Jeannie nods towards the guys' room. "Our fifth?"

"Bob's asleep now. He was sweaty last night. I don't think we'll go to Jim's."

He goes to phone the bank and Janet, Bob's business partner. Jean and Ange and I look at each other.

"You want me to stay with you?" asks Jean when Dale gets off the phone.

"Naaaah," he smiles like nothing's wrong. "Bob'll be alright. You guys go help the Carlsons."

We take turns in the shower while we listen for the phone. We hear Bob coughing in the bedroom.

The Carlsons call. They want to meet at Jim's about ten to clean out the apartment. We say OK, and plan to get there a half an hour early in case there's anything we need to "straighten up." Not that we expect to find anything shocking, but if we were to run across something, even a magazine or a poster, it might be nicer if the Carlsons didn't see it.

We leave Dale sitting at the kitchen table, his hands around his coffee mug. He looks lost. He looks the way he's going to look after Bob is gone.

We take the truck and stop by the grocery store to get a bunch of cartons. I've got the keys to Jim's place. When we walk up the steps I think of Jim standing there when I came by to drive him to the hospital. We climb the gray-mustard colored carpet of the stairs. The hallways smell like food. Living people still live here.

When I open the door to the apartment everything looks different. We set the empty boxes on the living room floor and begin to look in closets and drawers, intruding in a way we never would if Jim was around. There's nothing in Jim's drawers but socks and T-shirts and underwear, nothing beneath the bed but dust, stray pennies, a couple of crusty paintbrushes.

The Carlsons get there before we can go through all the rooms.

The Carlsons don't think there'll be anything they'll want from the living room, so I start packing the books and records, wrapping the TV in towels before I put it in a box.

Jeannie and Mrs. Carlson start in the kitchen. I hear Mrs. Carlson telling Jeannie about the first time Jim made scrambled eggs, about her trying to teach "my Jims," as she calls her husband and son, to cook. She laughs as she remembers the story of the eggs. It's good to hear her laugh. In Jim's room Mr. Carlson and Ange are packing shirts into cardboard cartons. I glance in. Mr. Carlson looks so small, like a schoolboy being sent away from home. He's very slow and careful as he fastens buttons and smooths collars and folds sleeves. He creases the shirts into neat, tidy rectangles. Ange says a couple of things but Mr. Carlson doesn't answer much. So after a while she leaves him to sort through his son's ties and loafers, his jackets and suits, his baseball things, alone.

"This must have been Scotty's room," says Mrs. Carlson.

I'd been in there when Scotty was around. But after Scotty, the door was never open.

The handle of the door is colored silver. Mrs. Carlson puts her hand on it. It clicks. She pushes it open. The curtain is drawn, the room is dark. But we can see around Mrs. Carlson, in front of us, that the bed and dresser and the night-table are gone. The only piece of furniture is the long desk by the window. The desk is crowded with clutter. There are pale gray-white rectangles on the walls. Ange flips on the light.

And all around is Scotty. Scotty in his red-checked lumber jacket. Scotty smiling with a three-days' growth of beard. Scotty sitting cross-legged on a mat. Scotty with long hair, a tie-dyed shirt, and sandals. Scotty in his ridiculous bright orange bermuda shorts. His firm brown stomach, his compact upper arms, him holding up a Stonewall fist and grinning. His fine hands holding something blue. His profile when he was a boy. Him resting his chin in his palms and looking sleepy. His baseball hat on backwards. His pretty shoulders, his tender sex, his hands.

In every one, his skin is tan, his body is whole, his eyes are blue and bright. We recognize some poses from old photographs, and some from Scotty as we remember him. But some are of a Scotty that we never saw; Jim's Scotty. Painted alive again by Jim.

"Dear Scotty," Mrs. Carlson says, "my Jim's beloved."

We take some stuff to a center that is starting up. We leave most of it in both their names. The TV in Scotty's. The hundred dollar bill in Jim's.

A few days later everything is over. The Carlsons are flying back to Texas. They don't want a ride to the airport but they invite us all down for coffee at their hotel. They tell us if we ever get to Texas to come see them. We all thank each other for everything and say if there's ever anything we can do. The Carlsons take some paintings to share with Scotty's family. When the airporter arrives we put their suitcases in the storage place beneath the bus. Mr. Carlson carries the paintings rolled up into tubes. When the bus pulls out Mrs.

Carlson waves to us for both of them. Mr. Carlson won't let go of the tubes.

We go back to Bob and Dale's and drink more coffee. We all get pretty buzzy. Then Jean says they shouldn't put it off anymore, they need to get back to Olympia. I mumble something about starting up temping again.

Jean says, uncharacteristically, "Oh, fuck temping."

Bob laughs. "Listen to that potty mouth."

Ange reminds me that I have to go back to Olympia to get my car, and I ought to help them finish the remodeling. Both of which are true, but it's also true they know what I can't say: how much I need to be with them.

So we say "See you 'round" to Bob and Dale and get in the truck to drive back down to Oly. Ange makes me sit in the middle, between the two of them.

"Wha-chew-wont, baby I got it!!" Ange howls as she shoves Aretha into the tape deck. Aretha takes a second to catch up with Ange, but then it's the two of them singing. Ange cranks the tunes up as Jean pulls the truck out onto 15th. We turn at Pine. Jean slows the truck as we pass the Rose in case anyone cute is casually lounging around outside; no one ever is. There's a moment of stillness at the red light on Broadway, a moment of stillness between the tracks, then "Chain of Fools." Ange cranks it up even more as we turn left onto Broadway, then turn right again onto Madison and right into a traffic jam.

Ange rolls down the window as if she needs the extra room to sing. She loves the chain-chain-chaaaaaain, chain-chain-chaaaaaain parts and always does this ridiculously unsexy jerk of her shoulders and hips when she sings it. She gets especially crazy at the cha-ya-ya-ya-ya-in part near the end. She squints and tries to look very mean, meaner with each ya-ya-ya. Jeannie is good at the hoo-hoo's, which she accompanies with some extremely precise nods of her chin, and some extremely cool finger points. I sit between them and laugh.

But as the song is nearing the end and we haven't moved more than ten yards, I growl, "What is this traffic shit?"

Ange pops the cassette out of the tape deck.

"What?"

"I said, what is this traffic shit."

"Quarter of four," says Jean, "I thought we'd miss it."

"The old 'burg ain't what it used to be baby. New folks movin' in all the time. And they all have six cars and they all love traffic jams. Reminds them of good ol' LA."

"Where they can all go back to in a goddamn handtruck, thank you very much."

We inch along a few minutes then come to a complete stop 'in front of Rex's. Pedestrians on the sidewalk look around for cops then start walking in between the cars. Someone squeezing by in front of the truck does a knock-knock on the hood and grins in at us.

"Smug asshole bastard," I snarl.

Cars start honking.

"Jesus this traffic sucks," I say louder.

Ange looks at me.

The car behind us is laying on the horn.

"Fuck the traffic," I shout.

"Hey, babe, take it easy," says Ange, "We'll get outta here soon."

I ignore her. "Fuck the traffic," I cry. I put my hands over my ears. "Fuck the traffic."

Then I hear Jim screaming, "Fuck the traffic! Don't they realize they're holding up a wheelchair full of dying faggot!" Then I hear him yelling, "So what am I supposed to do, fly?" Then he looks at me, "Tonto, I don't wanna, I don't wanna die."

Then my head is against the back of the seat. I'm rigid. Ange's hand is on my arm.

"Baby?"

Jean grinds the truck into reverse, backs up a couple inches, whacks it back into first and climbs over the sidewalk into the Seattle First National Bank parking lot. She cuts the engine.

"Baby." Ange says it hard.

She yanks me away from the back of the seat and throws her arms, her whole huge body around me. Jeannie grabs me from behind. I'm stiff. I'm like a statue. My body can't bend and I can't see. They sandwich me in between them. Spit and snot are on my face.

"Let it go, baby, let it go."

I can't say anything. My jaws are tight.

"Let it go, babe."

Ange pulls away from me enough to kiss my forehead. I break. She squeezes herself around me tight. Then they're both around me, holding me.

And then, dear Jim, held close between the bodies of our

friends, I see you.

I roll you and your wheelchair out to the sidewalk. I'm worried because in the few minutes it's taken us to get from your room to here, the sky has turned gray. I tell you we ought to get back inside, but you wave that idea away. I stand above you at the pedestrian crossing and look down at the top of your cap, the back of your neck, your shoulders.

There's a traffic jam. The cars are pressed so close not even pedestrians can squeeze through. A wind is picking up. People are opening umbrellas. Cars are honking, drivers are laying on their horns. I start to say again, that we really ought to go back in, but you find my hand on the wheelchair grip and cover it with your own. You sigh like a tolerant, tired parent. You shake your head. You pat my hand then squeeze it.

"The traffic'll break in a minute, Jim."

But you aren't listening to me. You slip your hand from mine, and before I can stop you, you've unhooked the tooth of the drip-feed from your arm.

"Jim, the IV."

"Ssssh." You put your finger to your lips like you are finally going to tell the truth about a story you've been telling for so long.

You slip the blanket off your knees. You stand up alone, not needing to lean on anyone. You're tall as you used to be. You stretch your arms out to your sides and take a deep breath. I see your chest expand. You stretch your neck up and look at the sky. You throw your arm around my shoulder and pull me to you. I feel the firmness of your body and smell the good clean smell of your healthy skin the way it was the summer we climbed Mt. Si. You pull my face in front of you. You hold my face between your hands and look at me. You look inside where I can't see, where I can't look away from you. Beneath the fear the covered love, you see me, Jim. Then, like a blessing that forgives me, and a healing benediction that will seal a promise true, you kiss my forehead.

You tell me, "Tonto, girl, I'm going for a ride."

You fling your Right-On Sister Stonewall fist up in the air then open your hand in a Hi-Yo Silver wave. I watch your hand as it stretches above you high, impossibly high. Your feet lift off the sidewalk and you rise. Above the crowded street, the hospital, above us all, you fly.

The rain begins. Cold drops hit my face when I look up at you. But you fly high above it, Jim. Your firm taut body catches glints of light from a sun that no one here below can see.

I raise a Right-On fist to answer you, but then my fist is opened, just like yours, and I am waving, Jim.

Good friend, true brother Jim, goodbye.

GRIEF

We're all at the airport to see our friend off to a foreign country none of us has been to before. Tonight there are hundreds of us. We all pitched in to buy the ticket. We bought her travel guides and sent her to Berlitz school. We traded evenings reading to her from phrase books and flash cards. We bought her luggage and clothes. We got letters of reference from well-connected people at home. We booked reservations for her in reliable hotels. We showed her our support. Though we're all reluctant to admit it, we live vicariously through her.

How did we choose her? Well, we didn't really. Like greatness, it was thrust upon her. The dubious honor of bringing us all together through our fear of departure.

Because beneath our party spirit, there's an edge. One thing's not arranged: her ticket home.

She stands at the gate to board the plane and we strain, from our distance at the end of the wide open hall behind the electronic surveillance gate, to see her face. She turns to wave goodbye to all of us and I have a flash of vision: I recognize this as a photograph we will show each other in the future when we remember her. I expect to hear a camera click, but I don't. Everything is quiet. None of us even breathes. She turns to walk into the collapsible corridor that leads to the plane when I notice she's the only person boarding the flight. It's then, and only then, I realize she's actually leaving. She throws her shoulders back with confidence. Her golden hair swings with her gait. When I hear something, it is the sound of her skirt rustling in air.

After we return home, only the bravest of us will allow herself to think we might not get postcards from her. We were so conscientious to give her all our addresses. Someone even gave her a telephone calling card. However, not even the bravest of us will admit what we think is true.

In the first few weeks she is gone, we tell ourselves she's too excited and busy to get in touch. She's having fun, we tell ourselves. We elaborate beautiful fantasies of the sunny streets she walks through, the sculpted gardens she spends her afternoons in, the exquisite dishes she dines on every warm exotic evening. We people her life with people we want to love us. Every dream we have we give to her. Some of us even envy her, so convinced we are that she has what we want.

But in fact, we hear nothing from her at all.

Gradually, we all think the same thing about her. We deal with this nobly, or rather, we deal with it with manners. It is one of the great, sad, tragic things that make us who we are. Our references to her grow vague, then disappear. We manage this transition without a word. But at home, alone, we each work hard at our forgetting. Here's what we forget:

We forget her hair. We forget the way it shone in the sun on the beach where we played in the summer. We forget the way she wore anklets and made us all laugh at her imitation of cartoon characters from our youth. We forget her milk-white complexion and the soft strong veins in her hands. We forget the dusty line of fuzz that covered the small of her back. We forget her small breasts inside her swimsuit. We forget the way her calves tightened when she crouched at the start of the city parks race. We forget the stories she told of her zany brother in the farm country. We forget the colored strips of cellophane she decorated her bedroom windows with so we could see the light make rainbows in the morning. We forget the warmth of her palms, the moisture of her hairline when she came home from a run. We forget the secret places she knew of when we were bored and couldn't think of anything to do. We forget the way she ordered sweet and sour pork and always, *always*, picked out the pork and only ate the sauce and vegetables. We forget the way she pushed back her hair from her forehead when she was trying to make a point. We forget her favorite song from her childhood. We forget the favorite shells she had collected from the northern shore when she went there with her family when she was eleven. We forget her annoying habit of never putting the toothpaste cap back on all the way and being obsessive about dust in her study. We forget her inability to compromise when her favorite program was on at the same time as a great movie. We forget the way she covered her mouth whenever she told a story she liked too much.

We forget in order to be happy.

That is why her lover, who forgets most of all of us, is happiest. She forgets things we never knew that, even if she wanted to, she couldn't tell us.

When most of the forgetting is done, something happens.

I get a call from her lover.

"I heard from her," she tells me. "She called me."

I can't say, "But that's impossible" without implying what we all think but don't say. Instead I say, "Oh, we'll have to hear about it."

I call several of us and say, "Her lover told me she heard from her. She thinks she got a phone call."

We agree it's a wrong number, a similar voice, even a cruel joke. We agree we don't need to do anything. Soon, we reason, her lover will forget the phone call.

But she calls me again. "I got another phone call from her. She says she's doing fine, but she misses us."

I call a meeting.

"She hasn't forgotten the phone call," I say. "She says

she's had another one."

"How do we know she didn't get a call?" someone asks.

We all turn. "That's impossible. It's imagination, just something she wants."

We decide to do something.

But we don't act fast enough. Her lover shows us a post-card she says she sent which says that she'll be home. The handwriting is faint and shaky. We must help our poor fool-ish sister through her grief by exposing her fantasy for what it is. So we pretend to agree with her in her expectation when she goes to the airport to meet the return flight. We all know she will not come back. We are not surprised when she does not arrive at the airport. But our poor, fool-ish sister is insistent. "She missed the flight," she tells us. "She'll be here." We go again. Again she isn't there. Again she says she missed the flight but will come back. We go again. Soon we go there all the time, forgetting we're only there to keep our poor sister company. Instead, we start thinking like her; we think she will return.

We show ourselves in huge numbers at the airport. We tell ourselves there's power in numbers. Even though we know we simply haven't got any power when it comes to this. We start re-enacting the past, hoping our re-creating can undo it. Over and over we re-live her final days with us, her departing flight. We stand where we were, we shout as we did. We try to do what we hadn't done then. The truth is, we never wanted her to go. We were afraid.

The past comes back to us, vivid as blood, how we tried

to soothe ourselves with final comforts. But all we did was give her guide books and feed her her favorite home-cooked meal the night before she left, throw her a farewell party. We vowed undying love and meant it, but learned that what we needed was forgetfulness, the only release from sorrow there is. And even now there is nothing we can do about our grief.

We stayed with her in vigils before she left. We told her we'd change places with her if we could; we couldn't. All our good intentions profited neither us nor her anything. All we could do was pretend — while she was with us — that she was coming back.

That's why we go to the airport in our party clothes. Why we sing Welcome Home as we remember pushing her toward her flight, why the cake we decorated says, "Welcome Back," why we refuse to sublet her room, why we refuse to offer help to her lover because we don't want to imply that she needs help, why we've left the bon voyage decorations up, the pink and yellow streamers, the cheery opaque balloons on the ceiling, the color-coordinated plastic forks and spoons, why we laugh and tell ourselves we're so clever to recycle them into Welcome Home.

We wander from gate to gate all the time. We stand and watch as flights deplane and people kiss their loved ones home. We mill around wearing our party hats and blowing our party favors. We offer punch and cookies to reunited couples, families, friends. "Welcome Home! Welcome

Home!" we cry, knowing the next flight will bring her back to us.

With our practiced songs and our party clothes, we make people happy. Especially her lover, because she is the most beautiful. She drapes her tan healthy body with light spring clothes, her arms and legs firm like a gorgeous young animal. In her bright green and blue and yellow silks, she smiles gracefully, but with the expectation of a confident child. Her longing for her lover's return, her nostalgia for every warm inch of her lover's flesh, is so strong we are almost afraid to be near her. She is flushed with the beauty of things about to happen. Her full, just parted lips, are ready.

We are sure she cannot have left us, sure she'll be back, sure she'll return even stronger and more beautiful than when she left. She will have braved something marvelous and strange. We are sure she'll enter with a flourish and tell us we were wrong to have remembered and forgotten what we did, to have ever stopped believing she'd come back.

But tonight, that's almost all I know, that I have stopped believing. It's not something anyone notices; my party hat is still on straight and my full lace skirt is crisp as starch. But I am singing our happy Welcome Home with only part of me. I imagine the sagging points of party hats, damp limp paper horns, ice cream turning to foamy puddles on paper plates, crumbs of lemon layer cake ground into the cracks between the linoleum tiles. Maybe the flush is weariness, not excitement.

In fact, I think I never believed that she'd come back. But I knew I needed something. I wanted to find it in all of us. I was warmed by our costumes and camraderie, our routines of ritual comfort. And, truly, I love the songs we sing together and the sweet look on people's faces at the airport when we give them cake and tell them about our friend.

But I didn't do these things because I thought she would return. I did them for us. And I did them in case, somehow, she could know. I did them to tell her that I would remember her. I did them to tell her goodbye.

The last memory I have of you, you're falling. Alone in the airplane corridor, you stumble. Your thin shoulders are hunched as though you're being pushed down. You can't bear to turn and look at us on your way out because you know what we'll see in your hopeless face.

The sound is your final gasp of air before you could tell us goodbye.